NOW

MORRIS GLEITZMAN

SQUARE
FISH

HENRY HOLT AND COMPANY

NEW YORK

For all the children
who never had the chance to do their best

**SQUARE
FISH**

An Imprint of Macmillan
175 Fifth Avenue
New York, NY 10010
macteenbooks.com

Library of Congress Cataloging-in-Publication Data
Gleitzman, Morris.
Now / Morris Gleitzman.
p.   cm.
Sequel to: Then.
Summary: While her physician-parents are working in Africa, eleven-year-old Zelda is
living with her grandfather, eighty-year-old Holocaust-survivor Felix Salinger, in
Australia, when a disaster leads them both to deal with unresolved feelings
about the first Zelda, Felix's childhood friend.
ISBN 978-1-250-03417-5 (paperback) / ISBN 978-0-8050-9713-9 (e-book)
1. Holocaust survivors—Juvenile fiction.   [1. Holocaust survivors—Fiction.
2. Grandfathers—Fiction.   3. Jews—Australia—Fiction.   4. Separation
(Psychology)—Fiction.   5. Wildfires—Fiction.   6. Australia—Fiction.]   I. Title.
PZ7.G4824No 2012   [Fic]—dc23   2011033496

Originally published in Australia in 2010 by Penguin Group (Australia).
First published in the United States by Henry Holt and Company
First Square Fish Edition: 2013
Square Fish logo designed by Filomena Tuosto

3 5 7 9 10 8 6 4

AR: 4.0 / LEXILE: HL610L

Now, at last.

It's arrived.

I can see it on the post office shelf.

Good on you, Australia Post, and your very kind pick-up counter that stores parcels instead of delivering them to grandfathers and spoiling their birthday surprises.

"That one there," I say to the man at the counter. "The one with my name on it."

I show him my homework exercise book to prove I'm me.

"Hmmm," says the man. "Zelda. Nice name, that. Daringly exotic and a bit unusual."

"Actually, it belongs to someone else," I say. "I got it secondhand."

"I know the feeling," says the man.

He points to his name tag, which says ELVIS.

We give each other sympathetic looks. Elvis hands me the parcel.

"There you go, secondhand Zelda," he says. "Hope it's something good."

"It's a present for my grandfather," I say. "He will be eighty tomorrow."

Elvis says something about how he wishes he was eighty so he could retire. I sympathize with him, but I'm not completely listening. At last I'm holding Felix's present, and I can't wait to give it to him. I can't wait for his big grin when he sees what it is.

Oops, I didn't mean to make an excited noise in the post office.

Calm down, Zelda, you're not a squeaky toy.

I thank Elvis and head for the door.

My phone beeps in my school bag. I know who it is without even looking.

Poor Felix. He gets worried if I'm late home from school. He's not used to being my substitute parent.

I text him back.

on my way see ya soon

I hug his present to my chest and hurry out of the post office. If I run fast and don't faint in this heat or trip over and fall into any ditches, I can be home in fifteen minutes.

But I don't get far.

"Hey, shorty," says an unfriendly voice. "Where's the fire?"

Three girls are blocking the street. They're older than me, thirteen or fourteen. Their uniforms are creased like they get into lots of fights and never do any ironing. The toughest-looking one's got a badge on her school bag that says CARMODY'S PEST REMOVAL.

She's looking at me like I'm the pest.

I don't know why. I've never met these girls before.

Escape plans flash through my head.

I could climb up the mobile phone tower on top of the post office, or I could dash round the back of the video store and through the fence and hide in the forest, or I could run into the bank and get a personal loan and buy a ticket to Africa on a flight that leaves in the next two or three seconds.

No, I couldn't.

"So," says the pest-removal girl. "Dr. Zelda, I presume?"

I try to work out what she means. And how she knows my name.

Adults are walking past, not even looking at us. Don't they realize that when three older kids are standing this close to a younger kid, it's not a social event?

"Hope we're not keeping you from a big medical emergency, Dr. Zelda," says the pest-removal girl.

Oh, okay. I get what she's on about. And it's my fault. A few days ago in class, when I was the new kid, Ms. Canny asked me to tell everyone about my family. I told them about my parents being devoted doctors in Africa and my grandfather being a retired brilliant surgeon.

I shouldn't have said brilliant. It's true, Felix is very brilliant, but it sounds like boasting. I should have said quite good or average.

"I'm on my way home," I say to the girl. "It's not a medical emergency."

"Yes it is," says one of the other girls. She points to the pest-removal girl. "Tonya needs medical attention. She's swallowed her gum."

I smile to show them I know that's a joke.

They don't smile back.

"Come on," says Tonya. "Cure me."

Lots of other kids walking home from school are stopping and staring now.

"Or is that stuff all lies?" says Tonya. "About your family being Australia's top medical geniuses."

"I never said that," I reply.

"My little brother's in your class, and he reckons you did," says Tonya. "Is that why you had to leave your last school, Dr. Zelda? Cause you make up stories?"

I don't know who her brother is, but he's wrong. He's

also lucky. I wish I had an older sister. Then she could help me explain to these three bullies the real reason I had to change schools.

More kids are gathering. Tonya grins.

"Dr. Zelda's new in town," she says to them. "We're all very excited. She's a medical genius. She can cure zits and bed wetting and do heart transplants."

I try to leave.

Tonya's bully friends drag me back.

"Not so fast, shorty," says Tonya. "What have you got there?"

I hold on to the parcel as tightly as I can. I might not be the biggest or toughest person in the world, but when I'm defending a precious birthday present, I can be very determined.

"None of your business," I say.

Tonya prods the parcel.

"You look nerdy, so it's probably a textbook," she says. "Let me guess. *Boasting for Dummies*."

A couple of kids snigger.

"It's for my grandfather," I say. "If you harm it, I'll tell the police you damaged the property of a senior citizen."

Tonya's face goes a bit uncertain. I should get away while I can, but I don't.

"I'll tell the local paper as well," I say. "It'll be front-page news, an eighty-year-old man having his birthday gift vandalized. And when I tell them who did it, your photos'll be on the front page too."

I stop, out of breath. I'm taking a risk, because I'm not sure if there is a local paper around here.

Tonya glances at the other kids. Some are looking uncomfortable. A few are moving away.

"What a storyteller," says Tonya. "Spellbinding. And mesmerizing. I'm totally entranced. No I'm not."

She grabs the parcel and yanks it out of my hands.

"Give it back," I say, lunging at her.

"Make me," says Tonya.

She ducks away and pushes past the kids and dances down the street. Her two friends go with her.

I run after them.

I know what I should be doing. I should be ringing the police.

But I haven't got time for phone calls.

Inside that parcel is something very rare and precious, and I think it's going to make Felix very happy, and I want it back now.

"**Now**," I say. "Give me that parcel back now."

Tonya has stopped on the riverbank. She's standing under the trees, panting.

I'm panting too. So are the other kids who've followed us. Nobody can run far in this heat, not with school bags, not even big kids.

"Zelda the storyteller," sneers Tonya. "Trying to impress everyone at her new school by boasting about her family. Pathetic."

"Give it back," I say.

"Only if you admit you're a liar," says Tonya loudly so the other kids can hear. "You can have your dumb grand-dad's dumb present back if you say you're a liar."

I won't say it because I'm not.

I have an idea. I take out my phone and find the text

Mum sent me a couple of days ago. The one about how the weather in Darfur is even hotter than here in Australia.

I take a step toward Tonya, holding out the phone.

"This is from Africa," I say. "From the clinic where my parents are working. Helping wounded children. They volunteered to do it. Nobody made them."

One of Tonya's bully friends grabs the phone and peers at it.

"Could be true," she says to Tonya. "If she was my kid, I'd run away to Africa."

I want to tell her that Mum and Dad didn't run away. They're so kind and compassionate and caring, they couldn't help going. But I don't say anything in case it sounds like more boasting.

Tonya is looking around. She sees she hasn't got much audience left. She raises her hand, and for an awful moment I think she's going to chuck Felix's present into the river.

But she doesn't, probably because in this heat there isn't any water.

She throws the parcel down near my feet.

Before I can pick it up, one of Tonya's bully friends grabs me round the neck. For the millionth time in my life, I wish I had a big sister. But I haven't. I don't blame Mum and Dad. They're too busy for more kids.

"Our turn," the bully girl says to Tonya.

For a moment, Tonya looks like she's going to tell them to leave me alone. Then she just shrugs.

The girl tightens her grip and hisses in my ear.

"We want more proof," she says. "If your grampy-pamps is a medical genius, prove it."

I don't know what to say. Felix is a medical genius, but how can you prove something like that with your head in someone's armpit? It's not like I can snap my fingers and one of Felix's ex-patients will stroll up and show them the amazing job Felix did on his bladder.

I need time to think, so I try to keep the girls talking.

"For a start," I say to them, "his name isn't Grampy-pamps."

I'm about to tell them his name isn't Grandpa either, or Granddad. When Felix was a kid hiding from the Nazi soldiers in World War II he had to use a fake name, and now he prefers people use his actual name whenever possible.

Before I can say any of that, the girl whose armpit I'm in grabs the little heart-shaped locket round my neck and pulls the chain tight.

I panic.

Whatever happens, I mustn't lose this locket. It's Felix's most precious possession, and he doesn't know I've got it.

"Leave it alone," I say.

"Why?" says the girl. "Is it from your boyfriend?"

The other girl sniggers.

"It belonged to a little kid," I say, "who was murdered."

The armpit girl blinks.

"By bullies," I say.

I glare at the girls to show them what I'm saying is true. Okay, it happened in 1942, but it's still true.

"You're right, Tonya," says the other girl. "She's a total liar."

"Totally," says the armpit girl. She yanks the locket off the chain.

I stagger away from her. I want to yell, but I see what the other girl has in her hand and my voice dries up.

It's something small and brown and furry. A dead bush mouse. Poor thing must have been killed by the heat.

I stare horrified as the girls stuff the locket into the mouth of the dead mouse. One of them grabs a stick and uses it to push the locket down the mouse's throat.

"No," I croak.

They throw the mouse at my feet. I can see the shape of the locket bulging in its little tummy.

"Don't worry, shorty," says the girl with the stick. "If Grampy-pamps is a medical genius, he'll know what to do."

Tonya comes over and punches the girl in the shoulder.

"Ow," says the girl. "What was that for?"

"You idiots always go too far," says Tonya.

"You started it," says the other girl.

"Use your brain," says Tonya. "We're trying to let people know there's a lying scumbag on the loose. They won't listen if you gross them out."

The three of them head off, arguing. The other kids who followed us are leaving too. I don't blame them. I wish I could go home myself.

But I can't.

Not without the locket.

Felix has treasured it for seventy years. It belonged to his best friend when he was a kid. Her name was Zelda too, and she was killed by the Nazis. Dad reckons she was the bravest six-year-old who ever lived.

Gently, I pick up the mouse and lay it on a rock. I open my school bag and take out my project scissors.

One cut is all it will take.

I hold the scissors like a knife. I tell myself it's just like slicing up meat for dinner. But it's not. Meat for dinner doesn't have little whiskers or soft brown fur.

I can't do it.

Somebody takes the scissors from me.

I look up, startled.

It's a boy.

At first I don't recognize him, but then I do. He's in my class. I can't remember his name but I remember his friendly face. He's in the science club, and sometimes when he breathes he makes a wheezing sound.

The boy slices open the mouse's tummy. Blood dribbles out, and tiny intestines.

I'm feeling hot and dizzy and sick.

I close my eyes.

When I open them again, the boy is crouched next to the tap in the picnic area. He comes back and gives me the locket and the scissors, both wet and clean.

"Thanks," I mumble.

He hands me my phone. The bully girls must have dropped it.

"Thanks," I say again.

"You okay?" he says.

I nod.

The boy gives me a concerned look. I get the feeling he wants to say something else, but he just wheezes for a moment, then hurries away.

I wait until my dizziness goes. Then I dig a small hole with my scissors and bury the mouse.

"Sorry," I whisper.

I don't cry. It wasn't so bad. Bullying can be much worse than this. I only had to survive half an hour. Poor

Felix was bullied by the Nazi army for most of his childhood.

I examine the locket. The gold color is dull and faded, but it was like that before. There isn't any real damage, which is a relief. You can still read the letters *F* and *Z* scratched inside it.

The metal link that connects the locket to the chain has come open, that's all. I put the locket back on the chain and close the link with my teeth.

I remember Felix's birthday present. I pick up the parcel. It isn't damaged either, which is also a relief.

I sit by the river for a while, feeling sad.

Sad for the mouse and sad for me.

There was something I didn't tell the kids in my new class. When I grow up, I want to be a doctor like Mum and Dad and Felix. So I can help people when they've been wounded by cruel illnesses or other people's cruel behavior.

Sometimes, to fix people, you have to be brave. You have to cut them open. Felix has done it heaps of times.

I hoped I could do it too, one day. I hoped I could be brave and fearless like Felix's friend Zelda was.

I think that's why Mum and Dad gave me her name. I think they hoped some of her bravery might rub off on me.

Which is why I secretly borrowed her locket. To see if it would.

But it hasn't.

I'll never be like the real Zelda.

And I'll never be a doctor. I'm not even brave enough to cut open a dead mouse. How could I help a sick person?

Now I'm nearly at the house and I'm feeling better.

Felix is so kind and loving, letting me share his comfy home and his beautiful trees and his unusual but mostly delicious meals.

Okay, I do feel a bit guilty about the bad thing I did.

Taking Zelda's locket without asking.

And yes, Mum and Dad would be horrified, probably with migraines. They explained years ago what Zelda's locket means to Felix. How it's the only thing of hers he's got left.

I agree I should have asked his permission, but I was too embarrassed.

I'll put it back carefully. And in a few years, when I'm brave enough to confess to Felix what I did, I think he'll understand how embarrassing it felt trying to get help from a dead person.

So I think it'll be okay.

My phone beeps in my school bag.

Probably another message from Felix wondering why I'm late. He's amazing. I only taught him how to text a few days ago. What a quick learner.

I get my phone out.

It's not Felix.

liar liar pants on fire no wonder
yr parents ditched u

A sick feeling jabs me in my cardiovascular system. I realize what's happened. The bully girls found my number on my phone.

I pull myself together and delete the text and head toward the house. On the way, I check myself in Felix's car mirror for signs of bullying.

Good. No bruises on my arms or neck, or rips in my school uniform. I don't want Felix to have his birthday spoiled with worry.

Jumble comes scrabbling round the side of the house to meet me.

He's the best dog in the world. His fur's a bit scratchy and his legs look like they're on back to front and he's fairly cross-eyed, but I love him. We've been friends for years and we've always wanted to live in the same house, and thirteen days ago our wish came true.

I pick him up and let him lick my face. He also licks my neck. Dogs don't need to see bruises to know when you've been bullied.

"Thanks," I whisper to Jumble. "Don't say anything to Felix."

I know he won't.

"Come on," I say as I put him down. "Let's give Felix his surprise."

I pause at the back door and glance down the hill because I'm having the scary thought that maybe the bully girls have followed me home.

No sign of them.

I don't think they have.

Felix opens the door. For a sec I'm not sure what's wrong. He's grinning, but his face looks sort of wobbly. Both his pairs of glasses are on the top of his head as usual, and they look like they're going to wobble off.

Then I realize nothing's wrong. It's just the air that's wobbling because Felix is holding a cake covered with burning candles.

I grin too.

Felix couldn't wait for his birthday tomorrow. I hope when I'm old I still want to do things right now this minute.

I start singing "Happy Birthday," and Jumble joins in. He can't do the words, or the tune, and he hasn't got much sense of rhythm, but he's the most enthusiastic barker I've ever had the pleasure of singing with.

"Hang on, babushka," says Felix, laughing. "This cake isn't for me. It's for you."

I stare at him, confused.

He knows my birthday's in August, not January.

I look closer and see what's written on the cake in icing letters.

CONGRATULATIONS ON FINISHING YOUR FIRST WEEK

AT YOUR NEW SCHOOL

That is such a nice thought. And I can see Felix did the icing himself because the letters are a bit wobbly from when his hands tremble sometimes.

"Thanks," I say.

My voice is a bit wobbly too, with emotion. It's what happens when you live with the best grandfather in the world as well as the best dog.

We go inside and I blow out the candles. Felix puts the cake down and I give him a big hug.

Oops, I forgot about his legs. But it's okay, he doesn't fall over. Poor Felix's legs are even worse than Jumble's. It was one of the awful things that happened to Felix when he was a kid. He had to hide from the Nazis in a hole in the ground for two years and didn't get to play any sports at all.

"So," says Felix gently, "was it a good first week?"

His face, which is old and a bit battered like his house, is smiling, but his eyes are watching me carefully.

I hug him again and keep my face pressed into his sweater while I think of something good to tell him. Felix always wears sweaters made from incredibly soft wool, even in summer. It's because he was cold a lot when he was young.

The feel of the wool against my face reminds me of the poor mouse's fur.

"Ms. Canny is nice," I say.

"Excellent," says Felix. "How many out of five are you giving her, Margaret?"

I smile at him. Sometimes we call each other David and Margaret, like the film reviewers on TV.

"I'm giving her four out of five, David," I say.

"I'm glad," says Felix. "Anything else you want to tell me about?"

There is, but I'm not going to. Instead I open my school bag and give Felix his present.

"Happy birthday," I say.

He looks surprised.

"I know it's not till tomorrow," I say. "But I can't wait."

Felix grins. "I can't either," he says, and starts ripping open the parcel.

I hold my breath. If he's grinning now, what will he do when he sees what's inside?

William's Happy Days by Richmal Crompton. The book Felix wants most in the whole world.

Mum and Dad have told me heaps of times how much pleasure Felix got from Richmal Crompton's William stories when he was a kid. Felix reckons that in a way they helped save his life. He's been collecting the William books ever since. Richmal Crompton wrote thirty-eight of them, and Felix has got thirty-seven.

Until now.

I bet when he sees *William's Happy Days*, he'll light up like a very happy Christmas tree and dance around the kitchen doing backflips like a very happy ballerina and hurtle through space showering sparks like a very happy space rocket.

Well, almost.

The wrapping tumbles to the floor. Felix flips his reading glasses down and stares at the book.

He's still grinning, but not quite as much as before.

I think he's in shock.

"Thank you, babushka," he says.

He kisses my cheek.

"You're amazing," he says. "Where did you . . . ?"

"I got it online," I say. "I had to search for ages."

I don't tell him it cost all my savings.

"Incredible," says Felix.

We go over to the Richmal Crompton bookcase. Felix

has loads of bookshelves all over the house. He lived in a bookshop when he was very little, and he reckons he caught books instead of measles.

The Richmal Crompton bookcase is his favorite one, which is why it's in the best position of all, next to the TV. We make a gap in a row of books and slide *William's Happy Days* in between number eleven in the series, *William the Bad*, and number thirteen, *William's Crowded Hours*.

Felix gazes at them. His eyes are slightly moist, which is what you'd expect when a person has finally got a full set of Richmal Cromptons after waiting eighty years.

He flips his glasses onto his head and gives me a big hug.

"This deserves a dance," he says.

We like dancing, me and Felix. It hurts him a bit, but he reckons he doesn't care because it makes him so happy.

I think it's probably the same when he thinks about the real Zelda.

Felix spins me away from the bookcase and around the room while he hums a traditional folk song from Poland, the sort of thing that was in the top forty when he was a kid.

After a while I do the special fast twirl he taught me last year. Except when he taught me, I didn't have anything in my pocket. So no locket went flying out of it and skidding across the floor.

Not like now.

We stop dancing and look at the small gleaming thing lying on the floorboards in the corner.

I feel sick, and my cardiovascular system hurts.

Felix goes over and picks up the locket. He stares at it, frowning.

"Where did you get this?" he says.

"The bottom drawer in the bathroom," I say in a small voice. "In that old matchbox where you hid it so burglars wouldn't find it."

Felix doesn't say anything, but he's frowning even more.

"I didn't know it was there," I say. "I was hunting for the nail clippers and I found it by accident."

I can't look at Felix, so I look at the floor.

"I'm sorry," I say. "I thought it would make me brave."

After a while I hear Felix sigh. Then he puts his hand on my shoulder.

"Let's have some cake," he says. He leads me to the table and we sit down. I've never felt so not hungry for cake in my whole life.

Felix looks at me. He has such kind, soft eyes, even when he's cross.

"You should have asked," he says. "But I forgive you, babushka. I know how scary it feels the first time your mum and dad go away."

I nod, because I can't speak, not just at the moment.

Calm down, Zelda, you're not a lawn sprinkler.

"It does get less scary," says Felix. "And they will be back."

He holds my hand while I cry. He's amazing. His mum and dad were murdered by the Nazis, and mine have gone for only three months, but he still knows how much I miss them.

"When my parents went," says Felix, "I wished I had something to make me braver too."

He puts the locket round my neck.

"Zelda would want you to have this," he says.

I still can't speak. I give him a grateful hug.

While Felix makes a pot of tea, I struggle with whether or not I should accept the locket. I would love to, but it's Felix's most precious thing.

I struggle some more while we have the cake. It's a carrot and zucchini and pumpkin and apple and raisin-and-bread-crumb cake with icing made from yogurt and marmalade.

Felix hates wasting leftovers. He hates wasting food of any description. He says that's how it is when there wasn't enough in your childhood.

The cake is delicious.

I have two pieces, and Jumble has three. He eats much too quickly, and as usual I have to whack him on the back when a mouthful goes down the wrong way.

Then I take the locket off and give it to Felix.

"Thanks," I say. "It's a really kind thought, but I've decided I don't need it anymore."

Felix looks at me, gives a little nod, and carries on chewing.

He understands.

He knows that lockets on their own can't make everything okay. No jewelry can.

It takes more than that.

Felix knows the secret.

So many sad things happened to him when he was a kid. Losing his best friend and his parents and the strength in his legs. And yet he's the happiest person I know. Because he's really good at doing happy things.

Reading books and making cakes and having hot baths and dancing.

Felix knows that as soon as bad things have happened, they're in the past. Which is the place to leave them.

From now on, I'm going to do what Felix does.

Leave the bad stuff in the past and concentrate on being happy now.

If I can.

Now. I want to wake up now.

I force my eyes open. I reach out and click the bedside lamp on. I'm hot and tangled and thumping and sweaty. My cheeks are wet and not just because Jumble is licking my face.

What a horrible dream.

It was dark. I couldn't move and they were coming. Thousands of them, marching in crumpled uniforms with pest-removal badges on their school bags.

I sit up and look at the bedside clock.

2:16 a.m.

"Are you all right?" says Felix, hurrying in.

He's wearing a sweater over his pajamas and his reading glasses are on his head and his hair is sticking up. He sits on the edge of my bed and holds my hand.

"You were moaning," he says. "You sounded terrified."

"It was just a bad dream," I mumble. "I'm sorry I woke you up."

"Don't worry about that, babushka," says Felix. "Anyway, I wasn't asleep. I was reading."

I stare at him. I wish I was allowed to read till 2:16 a.m.

"Are you sure you're all right?" says Felix.

I nod. Felix lets go of my hand.

"I'll be back," he says.

He hurries out.

Jumble sits next to me, panting hopefully. I can see he's thinking the same as me. Maybe Felix is getting us some hot chocolate. I'm pretty sure hot chocolate was invented to help people stop thinking about bad stuff.

Felix comes back. But not with hot chocolate. Instead he hangs something on the corner of the picture frame over my bed.

The locket.

"I thought you might like to have it just at night," he says.

"Thanks," I say.

It's a kind thought, and maybe he's right. Maybe it will help. I try not to show I'm feeling a bit disappointed about the hot chocolate.

Jumble doesn't even try. He whimpers mournfully.

Felix flips his glasses down and peers closely at the locket, which is gleaming in the light from the bedside lamp, but not very much.

"I'll have to give this a clean," he says. "Look how dull and tarnished it is from being in the bathroom drawer."

I feel a stab of guilt. I can't let Felix buy special metal polish for the wrong type of dullness and tarnishing.

"It might not have been from the bathroom drawer," I say nervously. "It might have been from the locket being inside an animal."

Felix blinks. "An animal?" he says.

"A bush mouse," I say. "A dead one."

Felix frowns.

"I'm really sorry," I say. "I tried to protect Zelda's locket, but I wasn't big and strong enough."

Felix looks at me for what feels like ages. Then he sits on my bed again.

"Babushka," he says gently. "Are you being bullied?"

I feel like kicking myself in the bum. I wasn't going to say anything about it till after his birthday. This is all my fault. I shouldn't try and have important conversations when I'm half asleep.

Felix sighs.

"I'm getting slow in my old age," he says. "I had an idea something was up yesterday afternoon, when I saw the way you were looking over your shoulder at the back door. I know that look. When I was your age, I looked over my shoulder a lot."

I sigh too.

Zelda, you're such a dope. How could you forget you're living with an expert?

Okay, Felix doesn't talk much about his childhood experiences of being bullied, but Mum and Dad have told me how often the Nazis did it.

"I am being bullied a bit," I say quietly to Felix. "I think it's because I'm new."

Felix nods.

"Do you think it'll stop?" he says.

"I hope so," I say.

I can hear in my voice I'm not sure.

Felix is still watching me. His soft eyes are sad and concerned. And suddenly I need to tell him about it. So I do. All of it.

He listens to every word.

"Felix," I say at the end. "If they don't stop, what should I do?"

Felix thinks for a moment.

"You need two things, babushka," he says. "A grown-up to tell, and a friend to watch your back."

He takes his glasses off and cleans them.

"You've got the grown-up," he says. "If these girls don't

stop, I'll have a word with them. Tell them what happened to some bullies I knew once who were arrested for war crimes and executed."

I look at Felix. I'm not sure if he realizes how big and tough Tonya is. I'll have to make sure if he has a word with her, he does it by phone.

"What about a friend?" says Felix. "Do you have one of those?"

I remember the boy from my class, crouching at the tap yesterday afternoon, washing my scissors.

"I think I might," I say.

"Good," says Felix.

I put my arms round him.

"Thank you," I whisper.

One day I want to be able to do what Felix does. Spot when somebody I love is having a problem and then help solve it.

I should be able to learn to do that because I am pretty observant.

"Hey," I say, pointing to the bedside clock, "it's after midnight. Happy birthday."

Felix grins.

"Thanks," he says. "Seeing as we're all awake, let's have hot chocolate."

I give a whoop.

That's the good thing about living on the top of a hill

in the bush with no other houses around. You can whoop loudly in the middle of the night, or even bark if you want to, and you don't wake any neighbors.

Felix stands up and rubs his legs and heads for the kitchen.

Jumble follows him.

I do too, but on the way, I stop outside Felix's room. His door is open, and I can see a book lying open on the bed. A book with a cover I recognize.

I go in and pick it up.

The book is old and battered. The edges of some of the pages are burnt. The words on the cover are in a foreign language. Felix had some jam from Poland once, and the words on the label looked a bit like this.

But this book isn't about jam.

I know this book. The picture on the cover is exactly the same as the English version.

William's Happy Days.

Inside the cover is a name written in pencil.

Wilhelm.

Where have I heard that name before?

I remember. Dad told me. It's the pretend name Felix called himself when he was hiding from the Nazis.

Felix must have had this book all these years. But instead of putting it on the bookshelf with all the others, he's kept it hidden away.

Why would he do that?

"Babushka," calls Felix from the kitchen, "do you want cake with your hot chocolate?"

I put the book down.

I haven't got time to solve the puzzle now.

But I will later.

After we've had our snack, Felix will need to get some sleep because he's got a big day tomorrow.

That'll give me the chance to get the English version of *William's Happy Days* off the bookshelf and have a read of it in bed.

Then maybe I can be like Felix and spot something that's bothering a person I love.

Now it's morning and something doesn't feel right.

I've got a book in my ear instead of a dog.

I sit up and I switch off the bedside lamp and put *William's Happy Days* under my pillow.

I'm the only one in the bed. Jumble must have got up early.

Hang on, I remember. Jumble went and slept in Felix's room because he was sick of me reading with the lamp on.

Not that I read very much. I conked out after the first story. It was good, but I couldn't spot anything in it that solved the puzzle about why Felix didn't want *William's Happy Days* on his bookshelf.

I'll read some more tonight. Today I've got too much to do. Starting with making a birthday breakfast.

I jump out of bed and grab the present Mum and Dad

left with me for Felix, and creep out of my room. With a bit of luck, Felix is still asleep and I can get the sweet-corn and banana pancakes made and then surprise him with them.

But Felix's door is open, and his bed is empty.

He and Jumble are already up. And I bet I know where they are.

I head out into the backyard.

I'm right. Felix is feeding the chickens. Well, not so much feeding them as standing there staring at them.

His shoulders are slumped and his head is bowed and he doesn't look like somebody who's having a happy birthday at all. He looks like somebody who's having a miserable birthday.

"Felix," I say, hurrying over, "are you okay?"

For a sec he looks startled. Then he grins.

"Eighty years old," he says. "Who'd have thought it? Do you realize I may only have another thirty years left?"

I try to work out if that's right, but it's too early in the morning.

The important thing is, Felix is grinning.

"Did you sleep better, babushka?" he says.

"Yes, thanks," I say. "Happy birthday."

I give him Mum and Dad's present. He starts to unwrap it, then remembers something.

"I got a text message from your mum and dad earlier," says Felix. "They send their love."

"Are they okay?" I say.

"Just a touch of nonspecific gastric mycosis," says Felix. "Apart from that, fit as fiddlers."

It's amazing their text got through. The phones in Darfur are very unreliable. And the computers. Sometimes Africa even gets power cuts in the hospitals. That's why Mum and Dad took flashlights.

Felix unwraps the present and holds it up and looks really pleased.

It's a sweater.

Mum and Dad give him one every year.

"Jumble's giving me the same as last year too," says Felix. "A swimming pool."

Jumble is in his hole, scrabbling at the dirt with his paws.

It's not really a swimming pool. It's Jumble trying to dig his way into the chicken pen. The hole's pretty deep for a little dog and getting wider. Sometimes Jumble needs help climbing out. Felix doesn't mind because the chicken wire goes a long way into the ground, and as Felix says, everyone needs a hobby.

"I'll make breakfast," I say. "Pancakes."

"Yippee," says Felix.

Jumble agrees.

"The taxi's coming to take us into the city at midday," says Felix. "So after breakfast, we've got time to go into town and get some birthday treats."

"Yippee," I say.

I was totally wrong about Felix having a miserable birthday. He must have been just feeling the heat. The temperature is pretty savage this morning, and it's not even eight o'clock.

In town we split up so we can surprise each other with birthday treats.

I take Jumble into the hardware shop to get something to clean Zelda's locket.

The hardware lady holds the locket up and squints at it.

"It's not real gold," she says.

"No," I say. "But it's very precious, so we'd like your best polish, please."

The lady gives the locket another professional stare.

"You say it's been inside a mouse?" she says.

I nod.

"Only briefly," I say.

While the lady gets the polish, Jumble tugs on his leash. He wants to show me something. It's a mechanical digger. I think he's dropping hints for when his birthday comes around.

We wait for Felix outside the shop.

My phone beeps with a text.

For an excited moment, I think Mum and Dad have got through twice in one day.

But they haven't.

zelda zelda worse than snot
u think ur special but ur not

I can feel my face burning. I erase the message and try to think about something else.

Maybe the friendly boy from my class is in town this morning. I hope so. Felix and Jumble could meet him. We could have iced chocolate together.

I peer up and down the main street.

No sign of him.

A little pang of loneliness stabs me in the respiratory system. For a sec I wish Mum and Dad weren't quite so kind and compassionate and caring. If they'd just sent some money to Darfur, or some syringes, we'd still be living in South Melbourne, and I'd be with my old friends.

Calm down, Zelda, no need to carry on like a social reject. Your old friends haven't forgotten you. Two of them called last week.

I look up and down the street again.

Still no sign of the boy.

Just Felix, waving as he walks toward us, carrying a bulging shopping bag.

That's weird, he's coming from the opposite direction of the cake shop.

I take the bag from him and peek inside.

This is even weirder. There are no cakes. Just some battered-looking carrots and some bits of cabbage and a lumpy vegetable I don't recognize. I take it out of the bag.

"It's a turnip," says Felix. "For my birthday soup."

I look at Felix to see if he's joking. A birthday soup should have special things in it, like mini sweet corn and fresh herbs and party frankfurters. This stuff looks more like chicken food. I know Felix likes to use up leftovers, but he doesn't normally use up other people's leftovers.

"It's a special soup I make on my birthday," says Felix. "To help me remember some special people."

Suddenly I understand.

It's a birthday soup from a long time ago.

Felix grins.

"Don't worry," he says. "I have cakes on my birthday too. We'll get them in a moment. First there's something special I want to get you."

Felix is amazing.

I bet there aren't many people with a scary wartime

childhood who can happily shop in an army surplus store. Surrounded by ammo belts and military knives and camping stoves that could be Nazi ones, for all we know.

It goes to show how good Felix is at leaving the bad things in the past and concentrating on happy things now.

Happy things like these boots he's buying me.

"Comfy?" says Felix.

"Brilliant," I say.

I stand up and walk around. They fit perfectly. The leather is really strong, but soft. The soles are really chunky, but light. They've got more lace holes than any shoes I've ever had.

Any bully would think twice about tormenting a kid who was wearing boots like these. The only thing I'm not sure about is why Felix is buying them for me. Today is his special day, not mine.

"Is this an early birthday present?" I say.

Felix shakes his head.

"I'm buying them because you need tough footwear here in the hills," he says. "And because a long time ago somebody gave me boots when I really needed them."

I give Felix a hug.

"Thank you," I say. "And thank you to that person."

"His name was Barney," says Felix softly.

I've heard that name. Mum and Dad have mentioned Barney.

I can hear in his voice that remembering Barney is making Felix feel a bit emotional. I look away toward the front of the shop to give Felix a private moment.

I'm glad I do.

I can see out through the shop window and across the street. To where three people are lounging against the front of the post office.

Tonya and her bully friends.

I duck down onto the floor behind a pile of blankets.

Felix is giving me a strange look. So is Jumble, who's been snoozing in a military helmet.

"These boots are very comfy for walking," I say to Felix. "I just want to see how they are for sitting."

I'm desperately trying to think of a way to keep us in the shop until Tonya and her friends move on. So Felix's birthday isn't ruined. If Tonya and Felix bump into each other, I wouldn't put it past Tonya to laugh at Felix's accent.

"Come and sit down," I say to Felix. "Tell me some stuff about Barney."

I know I shouldn't be encouraging Felix to dwell in the past, but I can't think of anything else. We haven't got a book to read together, and Felix doesn't like making up stories.

Felix sits on the floor next to me, groaning as he bends his knees.

He gets comfortable against the blankets and tells me about Barney, who was a dentist and who saved Felix's life and kept a lot of other children safe from the Nazis. Then he tells me about Genia, a Polish pig farmer who risked her life and her pig to hide Felix. And about Gabriek, Genia's husband, who looked after Felix for two years after Genia was killed.

These real-life stories are so gripping and amazing I'm not surprised Felix can't be bothered making up stories. I'll never think real-life stories are boring ever again. Or dentists, or pig farmers.

"Okay, babushka," says Felix. "Time to go."

I don't want to go yet. There's another special person I want Felix to tell me about. I've never heard him talk about her. Everything I know about her I've heard from Mum and Dad.

"Tell me some things about Zelda," I say.

"If we don't get home soon," says Felix, standing up slowly, "we'll miss our taxi to the city."

I've been so involved in the stories, I've forgotten to check if Tonya and her friends are still across the street.

I peer round the blankets.

"They've gone now," says Felix quietly. "The people you didn't want to see."

I stare at him in surprise.

He grins and helps me up. Which I need, because my legs have suddenly gone a bit weak.

"Are the boots comfy for sitting?" says Felix.

I nod.

"Good," he says, still grinning.

"Thanks, Felix," I say.

We look at each other.

He knows I'm not just talking about the boots.

Now I glance across at Felix in the taxi to see if he's okay.

He's been a bit quiet on the trip into the city, and I think he might be feeling stressed.

The taxi pulls up.

Felix definitely looks stressed.

I don't get it. When you've spent all your career being a really good surgeon and saving heaps of people's lives and about two hundred of them invite you to a gala birthday lunch at a big hotel so they can pay tribute to you and say thank you and show you how well their stitches have healed, you think you'd be happy, right?

Poor Felix isn't.

He's frowning like we're about to have a crash. And we're not. We're parked outside the hotel.

"This is the address, sir," says the taxi driver.

"Thank you," says Felix.

I can see he doesn't want to go inside.

"Are your legs hurting?" I whisper to him.

This is why we've come in a taxi. It's hard for Felix to drive all the way into the city these days because of his legs.

"Not too bad, thanks, Margaret," says Felix. "Three and a half."

If it's not his legs, what is it?

Perhaps it's the heat. The taxi driver said it's the hottest day for thirty years here in the city. But this taxi's air-conditioned, and the hotel will be too.

Whatever it is, it's not fair. A person should be allowed to do what he wants on his birthday.

"We could just go home," I say. "I'll make you a toasted sandwich with birthday sprinkles."

Felix looks tempted. But only for a moment.

"It's a very kind offer, babushka," he says. "But I agreed to this, and we must face our destiny with humility and resignation."

Sometimes Felix forgets that not everybody went to university for eleven years.

"Plus," he says, "there might be cakes."

The driver opens the door for us.

"Have a nice lunch, sir," he says.

"Thank you," says Felix.

The driver gives me a little bow.

"And you, Margaret," he says.

As soon as we walk into the hotel ballroom, I understand why Felix is feeling stressed.

The crowd is huge.

Everyone recognizes Felix and they jostle around us, talking excitedly and trying to get close to him.

Felix has spent most of his life away from crowds. There weren't any in his hiding hole, and after he left university, he spent nearly forty years in quiet operating rooms with only a few other people around, some of them unconscious.

No wonder big groups like this make him feel stressed. All these excited people hugging him and thanking him and showing him their children.

I hold Felix's hand so he knows I understand.

On the wall above us is a big banner that says HAPPY 80TH BIRTHDAY DR. SALINGER.

A man with a bow tie and a loud voice grabs Felix's arm and tells us all the details about the new digestive system he got from Felix twenty-seven years ago.

"Still going strong," he says.

That's a relief. For a sec I thought he was going to ask for another one.

A lady cries as she reminds Felix how he took a lump

of cancer out of her head when she was three. Poor thing. It must really hurt when you're that young.

"You're a saint," she says to Felix.

About fifty people say that.

He deserves it. I feel so proud of him. And I can see he's starting to relax as he asks everyone how they are and holds their hands gently in both of his.

It must feel so good to save sick kids and then meet them years later when they're grown up, with families and jobs and good health apart from a few back twinges and a bit of tooth decay.

I wish I could do that.

Felix introduces me to the last person he operated on before he retired. She's twenty-two now, and you can't tell she's got a false eye unless she taps it for you with her fingernail.

"Thanks," I say after she does it for me. "That's really amazing."

"Your grandfather's amazing," she says.

I agree.

A man about as elderly as Felix gives him a hug.

"Congratulations, old friend," says the man.

"Thank you, Miklos," says Felix.

I recognize the man and say hello. I met him once when Felix took me and Dad to a special survivors day at the Holocaust museum. I think he goes to the same Holocaust survivors group that Felix goes to.

While Felix talks to his friend, I look around the huge ballroom full of people, and a thought hits me. I remember a World War II photo I saw at the museum. A railway yard in Poland in 1942, completely empty after a Nazi death train had just left.

If Felix hadn't saved all these people's lives, right now this ballroom would be as empty as that.

I've never had lunch on a stage before.

Only six of us are sitting up here, Felix and me and four bosses from the children's hospital where Felix did most of his work.

The patients and their families and friends are sitting at tables on the dance floor, gazing adoringly up at Felix while they chew their lunch.

The hospital bosses are nice, and they're the ones who organized this whole event, so me and Felix don't say anything when the waiters bring our plates and we see what we're having.

Fish.

Felix doesn't eat fish. He liked it as a kid, but it gives him stomach cramps now. I know how he feels. I'm the same with bubblegum.

I give Felix a look to let him know I'll eat his fish when the others aren't watching.

My phone vibrates in my pocket. The short buzz you get with a text. I calculate it's four thirty a.m. in Darfur, so it's probably not from Mum and Dad.

It's probably one I won't want to read.

Instead I concentrate on the speeches.

One by one, people come up to the microphone on the stage and talk about how Felix saved their lives.

Felix is smiling, but I can see a sad look in his eyes, and I don't think it's about the fish.

Maybe he's thinking about Grandma and how she left him years ago and went to live in New Zealand because he used to spend so much time at the hospital with his patients.

I squeeze his hand a few times.

But on second thought, maybe it's not Grandma he's feeling sad about. She always sees him when she visits Melbourne, and they usually have a laugh.

A man wearing jeans and a leather jacket comes to the microphone. He starts his speech by describing how Felix fixed his throat after his windpipe got crushed by a rope twisted round his neck when he was nine.

Felix was a brilliant surgeon. I can see the man's neck from here. It's completely free of rope marks, and he's breathing normally through it and everything.

The man keeps talking even though the organizers have said one minute per person.

"Dr. Salinger knew I liked trees," says the man. "I think the climbing rope round my neck gave him a clue. So after the operation he said to me, 'Gary, would you like some trees to look at?' I said, 'Yes please.' So he asked the nurses to move my bed out onto the hospital balcony. But the nurses said they couldn't because it was against the rules. So Dr. Salinger bought cakes for all the nurses, and when they weren't looking, he moved my bed himself."

The hospital bosses at our table are frowning. I'm not sure if it's because they're worried this man's never going to stop, or because they didn't know about the bed on the balcony.

Felix has got his eyes closed.

The man comes over and puts his arm round Felix's shoulders.

"This bloke," says the man very loudly, "is a hero. Every child in Felix Salinger's life who needed help got it."

Everyone applauds. It's the loudest clapping of the day, on and on.

I'm so busy joining in that at first I don't see what Felix is doing. He's still got his eyes closed, but under the table he's clenching his hands so tightly his fingers are white.

I think I'm the only one who can see it. Even if I'm not, I'm probably the only one who knows why he's doing it.

It's his medical condition. Not his legs, his other one. Shaky hands. Lots of old people get it. You take pills for it, but you can never cure it completely.

It's tragic. Felix has spent his whole life helping people with his hands, and now his hands won't let him do that anymore.

He must feel so sad.

Hang on, that's it. Of course. That must be the answer to the *William's Happy Days* mystery.

I should have spotted it in the story I read last night. The story is about William doing things to help people. Rescuing an old man's penknife from the person who stole it, stuff like that. In one part, he has to pretend to be a dummy in a shop window. He has to stand totally still for ages, not moving a muscle, not even his hands.

Felix must feel so unhappy when he reads that story. It must remind him how his hands won't stop shaking. No wonder he didn't want that book on his bookshelf.

If only I'd known.

The clapping has stopped. Under the table Felix is still clenching his hands. And now two tears are rolling down his face.

Poor Felix.

I don't know what to do.

Felix takes some deep breaths and dries his eyes on his napkin.

"Sorry," he says to the people at our table. "It's okay, I'm fine."

He smiles at everyone, but his eyes are still red.

Everybody smiles back. I can see they think he's just feeling happy and tearful because of all the gratitude and how well everyone's stitches have healed.

They're wrong.

A person doesn't clench his hands like that out of happiness.

Now we're in the taxi and I'm going to say sorry to Felix about the book.

Right now.

I take a deep breath.

"Would you like some cheese?" I say. "Or a potato?"

Oops, that's not what I meant to say.

Felix is looking puzzled, so I quickly unfold the paper napkins in my lap and show him the leftovers I've saved from lunch.

"There's frozen chocolate cheesecake as well," I say. "It's melted a bit."

Felix smiles, but in a tired and weary sort of way.

"Thank you, babushka," he says. "I'll just have a piece of carrot."

He pops one into his mouth.

I pick up a cold potato, but I don't really want it. I've

got a lump in my stomach that feels like I've already swallowed it.

My phone buzzes in my pocket with another text. Whatever it says, I probably deserve it.

Suddenly I wish Tonya had taken *William's Happy Days* instead of the locket. And flung it under the wheels of a truck or put it in a blender or taken it out to sea and fired torpedoes at it.

Anything to stop me giving it to Felix.

Felix puts his arm round me.

"You're very brave," he says.

I look at him.

Does he mean the leftovers?

"That conversation you had with the other folk at our table," says Felix. "Not many people your age would be game to tell hospital bosses to stop wasting money on hair transplants and spend it on curing shaky hands and painful legs."

I don't know what to say. I did it while Felix was talking to some of his ex-patients, and I didn't think he'd heard.

"It wasn't that brave," I mumble.

"I think it was," says Felix.

He kisses me on the cheek. I force myself to be as brave as Felix thinks I am.

"Felix," I say, "I'm sorry I gave you that book."

I look at him anxiously. I hope I'm not upsetting him again by mentioning it.

Felix stares at me.

"I'm sorry it was a bad present," I say.

"Babushka," he says, "it was a lovely present. Don't think that."

"But," I say, "it made you sad and upset."

Felix looks like he's going to say it didn't.

Then he sighs.

"Yes," he says. "It did remind me of some sad things. But only a bit."

"It didn't look like only a bit," I say. "At lunch it looked like you were upset a lot."

Felix doesn't reply for a moment. When he does, his voice is very quiet.

"I got upset today because of what everyone was saying about me," he says. "I'm not a hero. I'm not a saint. I don't deserve to be called such things."

I gape at him.

I can't believe he's saying this.

Not a hero?

Try telling that to the man at the front table who was born with some of his heart missing and Felix fixed it up with tubes from the man's feet and bits of his bottom muscles.

"Felix," I say, "just because you're old and you can't

do operations anymore, that doesn't mean you're not a hero. You should be proud of what you've done. Heaps proud."

Felix gives me a sad smile.

"Thanks, babushka," he says. "But even when I was in my prime, I wasn't the hero everybody thought I was. In fact, people couldn't have been more wrong."

I don't get it.

Is Felix saying he's done bad things?

Impossible.

"Why were they wrong?" I say.

Felix stares out the taxi window.

"One day," he says, "when you're older, perhaps I'll be brave enough to tell you."

I think about this.

I decide not to ask him to tell me now, because it's his birthday and you shouldn't have to say things you don't want to on your birthday.

Anyway, I think I know already.

I know that when your parents go off and leave you, even when they love you and they've got a good reason to go, it makes you have a niggly feeling in the corner of your mind that maybe you're not good enough.

Poor Felix's parents left him for years and then, after the Nazis killed them, forever.

How could you feel like a hero after that?

But Felix is a hero, and he deserves to be proud and happy.

He just needs a bit of help.

The birthday present I gave him didn't help at all, so when we get home I'm going to give him something even better.

Now, one last check of the food to make sure I haven't forgotten anything.

Cheese sandwiches with tomato sauce faces.

Jam tarts with jam I made myself.

Lemonade with licorice straws.

A birthday cupcake in the shape of a hospital, with candles.

I'm glad I left Felix having an afternoon snooze in his armchair. It's good for him because in this heat he needs the sleep, and good for me because he can't see what I'm doing.

Laying out a surprise birthday tea for him in our favorite picnic spot in the forest.

I do a final check of the thank-you letters I've stuck to the branches around the clearing. Hundreds of them from hundreds of Felix's patients over the years. All real letters, not just texts or blogs. They look really good up there. Much better than stuffed away in that old folder in Felix's study.

I felt a bit guilty when I crept in to get them. It's the second time this week I've taken things without asking.

But I don't think Felix will mind. Not when he sees them flapping proudly in the breeze and I remind him how, since telephones were invented, only a very special person gets three hundred and seventy thank-you letters in his life.

He'll have to feel happy and proud of himself when he sees all this evidence. We'll probably end up doing dancing or cartwheels or something.

Okay, time to go and fetch Felix and Jumble before it gets too dark.

Hang on, what's that?

Over there, behind that bush.

Somebody watching me.

"Yes?" I say. "Can I help you?"

Oops, I didn't mean to say it out loud. I can't even see who the person is. It could be a bully. Or a council ranger. Or a picnic thief.

"G'day, Zelda," says the person, stepping out from the shadows.

It's the boy from my class who helped me with the bush mouse.

"Hello," I say.

The boy doesn't reply. He's gazing at the picnic. Particularly the tarts. This is probably the first time he's seen jam made from carrots, cabbage, and turnips.

I can see he thinks that it's a pretty good picnic tea. Specially the way I've spread it out on my bedroom curtain, even if the heat from the candles is making the licorice straws droop.

The boy looks up at the thank-you letters.

"Wow."

I think that's what he says, or else he might just be having trouble breathing.

I don't know what he wants, but I'm pleased he's here. For a sec I think of inviting him to the picnic.

Except I can't. Me and Felix have got personal things to talk about.

The boy peers at the candles.

"Is this a party?" he says.

"Yes," I say. "It's private."

The boy looks hurt.

I wish I hadn't said it that way. He's wheezing more loudly now.

"Are you okay?" I say.

"Yeah, thanks," says the boy. "Just a bit of asthma. Comes and goes. I'm used to it."

He must be. Some of the kids at school laugh at him when he wheezes, but he never cries or attacks them with classroom equipment.

"Ms. Canny calls me Puffing Billy," says the boy.

I give him a sympathetic look.

"In my family," I say, "we don't think that people should make unkind jokes about other people's medical conditions."

The boy looks at me earnestly.

"It's not unkind," he says. "Cause my name's not Billy, it's Josh."

He grins. I can't help smiling too. His face is one of the friendliest I've ever seen.

"Maybe I can help," I say. "My grandfather's got heaps of medical books. I could look up asthma and see if there are any cures your doctor doesn't know about."

"Really?" says Josh. "Thanks."

A sudden gust of hot breeze makes the candles flicker, and I remember I'm running out of picnic time.

"I have to go and get my grandfather and our dog now," I say. "If you hang around for a couple of minutes, I can introduce you."

Josh looks uncertain.

"I really just came to say sorry," he says.

I'm puzzled.

"Sorry?" I say.

"Sorry about my sister," he says. "I brought you this to apologize."

He holds something out to me. It's a T-shirt. It says CARMODY'S PEST REMOVAL.

I stare at it, stunned.

"Your sister is Tonya?" I say. "The bully girl?"

"Don't call her that," says Josh. "She's not usually like that. I dunno what got into her yesterday."

Suddenly I realize the danger I'm in. What if this is a trap? What if Tonya has sent him to distract me? Right now she and her friends could be creeping up, getting ready to wreck my picnic.

I peer anxiously at the shadowy forest. I can't see them, but bullies have probably had quite a lot of experience of creeping.

"Bring your grandfather over for a swim in our dam," says Josh. "When Tonya sees you're a friend of mine, she'll be really sorry she was mean to you."

As if.

I'm not that stupid.

"I can't," I say to him. "You have to go now."

My mind is racing. If the bullies are here already, watching me from behind the trees, I'm history. But if they aren't here yet, I might just be able to get the picnic safely back into the house.

"Tonya's not a bad person," says Josh. "Those two friends of hers are psycho, but she's not. Give her a chance."

"She didn't give me a chance," I say. "Now go."

I hate how unfriendly my voice is. But it's how you sound when you're being threatened by strangers.

Josh grabs my hand and stuffs the T-shirt into it.

"Take it," he says.

Desperately, I try to pull my hand away. But he's holding on too tight. I yank my arm even harder. It gets hooked in the T-shirt. Josh stumbles forward and bangs into me, and we both fall over.

I scramble to my feet, ready to dodge away if he tries to grab me again.

But Josh is on his feet as well, running off into the forest.

As the sound of his wheezing fades, I crouch down, trembling, my arm throbbing. I listen for other sounds.

Sniggering.

Sneering.

The squeaks of bush mice being captured and killed.

But there isn't anything like that.

Just a strange crackling sound behind me.

I turn round.

And stare in horror.

Flames are rushing up the bark of one of the trees. Tufts of grass are on fire. At first I don't understand what's going on.

Then I do.

Struggling with Josh, I must have knocked a candle over.

I grab my bedroom curtain, food flying everywhere, and use it to try to beat the flames out. But it's no good. Everything is so dry and the hot breeze is stronger now and one of Felix's thank-you letters is alight and now the flames are leaping from letter to letter.

I snatch the lemonade and soak my curtain with it and beat at the flames on the ground and the ones on the tree trunks. My arms are killing me, and my eyes are stinging, and my throat is rasping as I swipe and stamp and desperately try to smother the flames.

On and on till gradually the grass is just smoking and the bark is just black and I'm on my knees, gasping for air and shaking so much I can hardly hold the curtain.

I smother the grass some more until it's not even smoking, and I peer at the tree trunks to make sure there are no more flames. Then I roll onto my back and take some big breaths and try not to think how close I came to causing a huge disaster.

After some deep breathing, I start to calm down.

But not for long.

The blurriness in my eyes clears, and suddenly I see some flames I've missed.

I jump up, frantic, but there's no point.

There's nothing I can do.

High above me, swirling gracefully in the breeze and floating away into the dark sky, are hundreds of burning thank-you letters.

Now. I have to tell Felix so that he can phone the fire brigade now. And the state emergency service. And a lawyer in case I get arrested.

I sprint through the dark trees and into the front yard.

Jumble comes round the side of the house to meet me. He jumps up and wags his tail. He probably wouldn't be so welcoming if he knew what I've done.

"Sorry, Jumble," I say. "It's an emergency. I think I've started a bushfire."

I rush to the front door.

Before I can go in, something catches my eye.

Through the living-room window, I can see Felix in his armchair. He's sitting forward with his head in his hands.

Does he already know?

Then I see he's not alone. Several people are sitting with him. One person has a hand on his arm.

My thoughts swirl like burning bits of paper.

Is Felix being questioned by the arson squad? Plain-clothes investigators whose job is to track down firebugs and make sure they get seriously punished?

I duck down onto the veranda.

I have a strong urge to creep away into the forest and hide there for years. Except Felix lived in a forest once when he was a kid, and he reckons it's really hard finding enough to eat. One birthday picnic tea wouldn't last long.

Anyway, get real, Zelda. You can't hide in a forest if you've set fire to it.

I peek through the window again to see if Felix is okay. I can't leave him at the mercy of the investigators. I have to go in and confess.

Then I recognize the person sitting next to Felix. It's the man from the Holocaust survivors group I met at lunch.

I look closely at the other people. They don't look much like arson squad investigators either. They're all elderly, and they're watching Felix like they're concerned about him rather than interrogating him.

I realize what must have happened.

The survivors group must have dropped in as a birth-day surprise.

Felix looks up and sees me and waves. I wave back, and move away from the window.

Mum and Dad explained to me how important the survivors group is to Felix, and how private. When you've been very seriously bullied, there are sad things you can only say to other people who've also been very seriously bullied too, because only they really understand what you're talking about.

I hope Felix can tell them how he's feeling. Including the reason he doesn't think he's a hero. So they can tell him he's wrong and cheer him up.

I don't have time to do it at the moment.

I've got a fire to worry about.

I get a flashlight from the car and hurry back into the forest with Jumble.

He and I can phone the fire brigade ourselves if we have to.

I look around for flames.

I listen for the crackle of burning.

I ask Jumble to sniff for smoke. He does in several places, including down a couple of wombat holes.

Nothing.

Just dark trees all around us, sighing and groaning in the hot breeze.

I pick up Jumble and give him a relieved hug.

"Maybe I was wrong about the fire," I say.

He licks my face.

There must be a chemical in dog saliva that helps you think more clearly, because suddenly I know what I should do.

Be like Felix.

Don't dwell on the bad stuff.

Wait and see if there actually is a fire, rather than jumping the gun and panicking everybody.

"Thanks," I say to Jumble. "That's really good advice. Come on, let's go and see what's happened to the birthday picnic."

When I get back to the house, the visitors are leaving.

I ask Felix to put his fingers in his ears.

"Would you all like to share Felix's surprise birthday picnic tea?" I whisper to the visitors.

They say that's very kind, but no thanks because it's getting late and they have to go all the way back to the city.

"I understand," I say. "Thanks for visiting Felix on his birthday."

After they've gone, I ask Felix to put his hands over his eyes. I go out to the carport and get the picnic and lay it out on the living-room floor.

"Wow," says Felix when he's allowed to look. "That is the best birthday picnic ever."

I can see Jumble agrees.

We have the picnic.

"Clever idea," says Felix. "On a hot day like today, very smart idea to wait till evening and have the picnic in front of the fan. You've got a great future in the birthday tea industry, babushka."

He gives me a grin. He seems much happier after his chat with the survivors.

I manage to grin back.

Some of the sandwiches have got twigs in them, and the cake hospital is a bit demolished, and the jam tarts smell of smoke. But Felix doesn't seem to have noticed. Or if he has, he's not saying anything because he's so kind.

I wish I could give him another birthday hug, except I don't want him to notice I smell of smoke too. And I don't want him to feel how stressed I am.

It's very hard, not dwelling on the bad stuff.

I keep glancing at the TV news for pictures of flames. And I'm listening for the distant sound of fire trucks.

I tell myself everything's okay. That there's no need to alarm Felix on his birthday. No need to upset him with the news that his granddaughter is an idiot who lights candles out of doors during a total fire ban.

Except if everything's okay, why are my hands so sweaty, and why is my head thumping, and why is my cardio-vascular system beating so fast?

Calm down, Zelda, you're not a fire alarm.

I'm cleaning my teeth.

I shouldn't be.

I shouldn't even be in the bathroom. I should be up on the roof, checking the horizon. Keeping my eyes peeled for glowing embers.

Flickering flames.

Huge exploding fireballs.

And while I'm up there, I should ring the fire brigade and tell them I've set fire to bulk correspondence and probably started hundreds of fires all over the state.

Instead I rinse my toothbrush and give myself a long look in the mirror.

You're a panic merchant, Zelda. Dad's always saying so. He reckons it's because you've grown up with people talking so much about hospitals and operations and war.

I tell myself to calm down.

It's the middle of summer. Everyone's on bushfire alert. It was on the news. The moment a burning thank-you letter lands in their backyard, people will be sloshing water onto it and spraying foam at it and smothering it with wet blankets and bulldozers.

It'll be fine.

I nod so my reflection knows it definitely will. But my reflection doesn't get the message. She looks like she's being strangled.

To get my mind off things, I take Zelda's locket and the bottle of metal polish out of the bathroom drawer. I grab some toilet paper and clean the locket till it shines. Then I hang it on the towel rack.

It looks good.

Felix will see it when he comes in for his bath.

The last of his happy birthday surprises.

As I step quietly out of the bathroom, I have a little pang of jealousy. Felix is lucky. Each evening when he has a bath, he gets happy memories of all the bathtimes he had with his parents when he was little. I've tried doing the same, but it didn't work for me. Probably because we mostly had showers at home. I don't think showers are as good for memories. Maybe that's why Felix prefers baths.

Felix comes out of his room in his bathrobe.

"Nighty night, babushka," he says. "Thanks for a lovely birthday."

"You're welcome," I say.

He blows me a kiss and goes into the bathroom.

I wish I could just collapse into bed and forget the whole day. But I can't. My cardiovascular system won't let me.

I don't care how much people slosh and spray and totally smother Felix's thank-you letters with bulldozers, I won't get to sleep until I check properly that there are no fires.

I go into my room.

Jumble is on the bed. He looks at me sleepily.

"Nighty night," I say, patting him. "Don't wait up. There's something I have to do before I come to bed."

I can see he understands because he thumps his tail a couple of times and puts his head inside my school bag.

I creep out of the house.

Now, Felix's ladder.

I think he keeps it in the carport.

Yes, here it is.

Okay, Zelda, quietly. Don't demolish anything.

The ladder is heavy, but I manage to carry it over to the side of the house without banging into stuff, and after a bit of wrestling, I get it propped up against the gutter.

I know I shouldn't be doing this without somebody to hold the ladder steady, but I haven't got anybody.

Anyway, Mum and Dad told me how when Felix was a kid, after he left his hiding hole, he spent some time helping Jewish partisans fight the Nazis, and I bet Felix didn't have people to hold things steady for him the whole time.

I climb up the ladder and slither onto the roof.

It's been dark for hours, but the sheets of metal are still warm. Crouching for balance, I waddle up the slope to the chimney and hang on to the bricks and peer around at the horizon.

The sky is clear and the moon is out and all I can see are dark treetops.

There isn't a single glimmer of fire anywhere.

I'm trembling with relief.

It's pretty good up here. It's like I'm sailing on a sea of trees. No, I'm on the deck of a spaceship, hovering over a planet totally covered with giant broccoli.

I close my eyes and imagine the warm breeze is gently wafting all my worry and stress away, away, away beyond the farthest trees to the town tip.

I sigh contentedly.

Then I smell smoke.

My eyes snap open and I peer into the distance for the leaping flames I've missed.

Nothing.

"Hope you've got a stethoscope up there, Dr. Zelda," says an unfriendly voice, loud in the darkness. "You'll need it if you fall off."

My insides give such a jolt I almost do fall off.

Tonya.

I see her, standing inside the front gate with her friends, three shadowy figures in the moonlight, each one with a glowing cigarette.

"What do you want?" I say.

I have a crazy hope that Josh was right. That she wants to apologize.

But the way she's standing, with one hand on her hip, isn't the way people stand when they're saying sorry.

"My brother reckons you're gonna get his asthma cured," says Tonya. "I just want to know if you're telling the truth or if he's going to end up sad and disappointed."

Her tone of voice sounds like she thinks Josh will probably end up sad and disappointed. And like she wants to make me suffer for it now.

Before I can reply, a light comes on and Felix hurries out of the house in his pajamas and birthday sweater.

"What's this?" he says to the girls.

"Just having a chat with your granddaughter," says Tonya, glaring at me.

Felix peers up at me. His mouth falls open.

"Babushka," he says, "what are you doing? Are you all right?"

"Don't worry," I say. "I'm fine."

That's not completely true. My bare feet are starting to sweat, and I can feel them getting a bit slippery.

"Are you the old granddad that cures people?" says Tonya to Felix.

Felix doesn't answer for a while, just keeps looking at me like he's trying to work out why I'm up here. Then he turns to Tonya.

"If you don't put those cigarettes out," he says, "I'll be the old granddad who turns the hose on you. There's a total fire ban."

Even though the night air is hot, I can feel myself blushing.

The girls stub out their cigarettes.

"I used to be a surgeon," says Felix. "But I'm retired. I haven't treated anybody for fourteen years. If it's urgent, I can take you to the hospital in town."

Tonya doesn't answer.

Instead she glares up at me.

"Typical," she says. "Zelda the lying storyteller. You should be locked up. With a tattoo on your head that says liar. Vermin like you are a menace."

Tonya turns to leave.

Before she can, Felix grabs her by the shoulders.

"Locked up?" he says. "Vermin? Can you hear yourself? People die because of stupid, vicious talk like that."

She looks at him, stunned.

He starts shaking her.

"Innocent children," he shouts. "Murdered. Don't you know anything?"

I stare down at Felix in shock.

I've never seen him do a single violent thing in my whole life. And now he's lifting his hand as if he's going to hit Tonya.

"Felix," I yell. "Don't."

He looks up.

For a moment, he doesn't even seem to recognize me. Then his face goes sort of limp. He lets go of Tonya, who staggers backward, swears at him, and runs off with her friends.

Felix stands there, his arms hanging like floppy ropes.

He looks like he's going to cry.

I scramble down the ladder as fast as I can, my sweaty feet slipping on the rungs. My thoughts are slippery too, and I can't get hold of them.

Felix has never done anything like this before.

He told me once that a surgeon has to be able to control his emotions. But he wasn't controlling them just then.

It was like something was controlling him.

Now that I'm down the ladder, I can see how badly Felix is trembling.

Panic flares up inside me. He's breathing very fast and he looks like he's in pain. What if poor Felix is having some sort of stroke?

I'm no good with medical emergencies.

Frantically I try to work out what time it is in Darfur and whether Mum and Dad can get on a plane and fly home now or whether they'll have to finish sewing up kids first.

"I'm okay, babushka," says Felix. "I just need to lie down for a moment."

I give up on the calculation and help him indoors.

He flops down on his bed.

I get Felix a glass of water and a jam tart. When I come

back from the kitchen he's just lying there staring at the ceiling.

At least he's not shaking now, and his breathing seems back to normal.

"That was unforgiveable," says Felix.

I sit on the edge of his bed and hold his hand.

"It's okay," I say. "I don't really mind. They're just big bullies. They don't mean half of what they come out with."

Felix keeps staring at the ceiling.

"I'm talking about me," he says quietly. "The way I behaved. I'm ashamed of myself."

I give him the jam tart to show him he doesn't have to be. Not ever.

"You were standing up for me," I say.

Felix looks at me. He opens his mouth to say something, then closes it again.

"Don't feel bad," I say. "Even brilliant surgeons can't be expected to control their emotions all the time. If you did, how could you enjoy watching cricket or reading scary stories?"

Felix frowns. He looks like he's having lots of thoughts. I hope they're about how whatever's troubling him can wait till tomorrow. How it all won't seem so bad after a good night's rest.

Felix does a big sigh.

"I need to go to sleep now, babushka," he says.

I kiss him on the cheek.

"Sleep tight," I whisper.

"And you," he says.

"Jumble," I murmur, "be quiet."

I open my eyes.

I'm in bed in the dark, and now that I've started waking up, I'm realizing where the noise is coming from.

It's not Jumble, even though he's asleep with his nose in my ear. It's Felix, calling from his room. He's calling my name, and he sounds really upset.

I sit up.

Jumble gives a startled yelp and falls into my lap. I pick him up and scramble out of bed still half asleep and hurry into Felix's room.

Felix's bedside lamp is on as usual because he hates the dark.

"Felix," I say, "what's wrong?"

He doesn't answer. I can see he's still asleep.

"Zelda," he moans. "Zelda."

"It's okay," I say, giving him a gentle shake. "I'm here."

Felix opens his eyes and sees me and sort of blinks with the look he gets when he eats gherkins too fast.

I kneel by his bed and give him a hug. His breath has a sleepy smell, but it's no worse than Jumble's. Anyway, I don't care because he needs a hug. I've never seen him looking so unhappy.

"Was it a bad dream?" I say.

Felix sighs.

"Horrible, Margaret," he says. "I'm giving it a zero."

Poor Felix.

He's not used to bad dreams. Mum reckons he hardly ever has them. Which is pretty amazing for someone who was shot at as a kid and has seen hundreds of people's insides.

I squeeze his hand.

"At least I was in the dream with you," I say. "Keeping you company."

Felix gives me a look, like there's something he wants to say, but he's not sure how to say it.

I notice something peeping out from under the edge of his pillow.

The locket.

I am such a dope.

Now I'm awake properly, of course I know it wasn't me in Felix's dream. For a start, he never calls me Zelda. I don't think he realizes he doesn't, but I know that name is reserved for someone else. I think Felix probably wishes

Mum and Dad hadn't given it to me. How confusing must it be, having two people you care about both with the same name?

"I was dreaming about a long time ago," says Felix quietly.

I nod.

I know.

I'm not surprised.

When Mum and Dad started telling me things about Felix's childhood, I looked at stuff online about World War II and the Holocaust, and I saw photos of Jewish people being starved and killed.

Children lying dead on the ground with people just stepping over them.

How can anyone not have sad dreams with memories like that?

Felix sighs again.

I want to let him know it's natural to have sad dreams when people you love aren't around anymore. I do it all the time.

"Zelda was your best friend," I say.

Felix nods.

I wish he'd tell me about her. I think it would help him if he could talk about her sometimes.

"She must have been very special," I say to him.

Felix looks at me as if he's not sure what to say.

Then he tells me just how special she was. And funny. And really good at drawing. How she helped him survive the war. How her loving spirit has inspired him to do everything he's done in his life since.

Stuff like that.

I can't concentrate on all the details. Part of me has to concentrate on trying not to feel jealous.

"I wish they hadn't given you her name," says Felix. "Your parents did it as a gift to me, but it's not fair on you, babushka."

I agree.

I reckon you should only be given a person's name if your parents think you're as clever and brave and special as the original person was.

But I don't say that to Felix because it isn't his fault his best friend is so impossible to live up to.

"You must really miss her," I say.

Felix nods. He has the miserable look he had in the taxi when he told me he wasn't a hero.

"I miss her a lot," he says, "but there's something else as well."

He struggles to say more.

The words won't come out.

Poor Felix. Something is torturing him. I wish I could

help. But I'm not up to it. When I try to help people, trees die.

I can't get back to sleep.

Jumble is trying to relax me by licking my face. Usually that helps a lot. I think dog saliva must have a relaxing chemical in it, because usually I go to sleep very quickly when he does that.

But not now. My legs won't stop wriggling and the sheets are getting all tangled.

I can't stop worrying about Felix. About how he got so upset with Tonya he almost hit her.

I don't get it.

Felix has spent his whole life healing, not hitting.

So what made him do that? What made him flare up like a bunch of thank-you letters in a hot wind? Can grief and sadness from seventy years ago make a person do that, or is it something else?

I sit up in bed and tell myself to calm down and stop carrying on like a forensic psychologist.

I met a forensic psychologist at one of Mum and Dad's barbecues, and he had dark rings round his eyes like he hardly ever slept.

I think I'm getting those rings.

Or maybe it's just dried dog saliva.

If only Mum and Dad were here. Then I could ask their advice about how to help Felix. And after they had given it to me, Mum could help me get to sleep by stroking my head like she used to when I was little.

I decide to ring them.

I check the world clock on my phone.

It's 7:43 p.m. in Darfur. Even dedicated doctors who devote all their time to healing wounded kids probably knock off by 7:43 p.m.

I ring the African clinic using the Médecins Sans Frontières number that Mum and Dad left me in case of an emergency.

This is definitely an emergency.

Please answer.

But all I can hear is a very faint recorded message in a foreign language, then beeping whistling sounds.

I send Mum and Dad a text.

i need 2 talk r u there

I wait for a reply.

One doesn't come.

I sigh.

For the millionth time in my life, I wish I had a sister. Someone to keep me company and give me advice.

But I don't.

It's just me.

Jumble is nuzzling me and whimpering in my ear. For a sec I think he's telling me he's suffering from insomnia too. But the way he's looking at me with his eyes big and caring, and the way he's panting in a very loyal way, makes me realize what he means.

"I'll be your sister," he's saying.

I put my arms round him.

"Thanks, Jumble," I say. "You and me. We'll look after each other, and Felix."

Jumble sticks his tongue up my nose, which I think is his way of saying, "Yes, and we'll do a really good job."

My phone beeps.

It's a text.

Mum and Dad must have replied.

I grope under the sheets, and Jumble helps me find the phone. If I had a tail, I'd be wagging it with excitement like him.

I read the message.

yr hole family shd b locked up

I snap the phone off and flop back onto my bed.

I'm glad Jumble can't read.

Even though he definitely can't, he still knows how disappointed I feel.

I can tell because he's licking my eyelids. And thumping his tail on the bed impatiently.

In the distance I hear the rumble of thunder.

Of course.

There definitely must be something in dog saliva that helps you put two and two together and get the right answer, because I realize what Jumble is telling me.

He's letting me know that at least I don't have to worry about the fire.

A storm is coming.

Rain, drenching the forest, swooshing across the countryside, extinguishing every last dangerous glowing ember.

I give Jumble another big hug.

"Thanks," I say.

He's the best sister I've ever had.

Now I'm roasting.

Turn the heater off, someone, please.

I sit up in bed, blinking in the morning sunlight that's searing into my room. I grope for the curtain to block it out.

No curtain.

I remember why. It's in charred scraps at the picnic place in the forest.

I also remember there's no heater in my room. It's the middle of summer. All the heaters are stored under the house.

I peer at my bedside clock.

This is incredible.

It's only seven thirty in the morning, and it must be another heat record already.

Poor Jumble is panting. He needs a drink.

So do I.

"Come on," I say. "Race you to the tap."

Felix's bedroom door is open, and I pause in the doorway to see if he wants a drink too. But he's not there. He must be up already.

I see something else.

Lying on Felix's bed is his bathrobe and the Polish copy of *William's Happy Days*.

A thought hits me.

Felix likes to read in the bath.

He was probably reading *William's Happy Days* last night while I was up on the roof.

Is there another upsetting part in this book? Is that why Felix got so upset with Tonya and then had a bad dream about the first Zelda?

I go into Felix's room, pick up the book, and turn the pages. Which is pointless as it's all in Polish and I don't understand a word. I'll have to hurry up and read the rest of the English copy.

As I'm closing the Polish book, I see something inside the back cover that I do understand.

A drawing in pencil that looks like it was done by a little kid. Two people and what looks like some chickens. I think they're all dancing. Under one person is the letter *F*, and under the other is the letter *Z*.

Just like what's scratched inside Zelda's locket.

I stare at the two stick people, who are holding hands. Is that why Felix didn't put this book on the bookshelf? Because it's got a drawing by Zelda in it?

Jumble gives a loud whimper.

I remember how thirsty we are.

"Sorry," I say to him, putting the book back on the bed.

Then I smell it.

Smoke.

Jumble whimpers again. Dogs are really good smoke detectors. They could do it for a living if they could learn to hang from the ceiling.

Panic flickers inside me as we head toward the kitchen.

Please just let it be Felix making toast.

But Felix isn't in the kitchen. The toaster is switched off. Through the kitchen window I can see the ladder up against this side of the house where I left it last night. And near the top of the ladder, Felix's feet.

I give Jumble some water, gulp some myself, and hurry outside.

Felix is up the ladder, scooping leaves out of the gutters.

He shouldn't be, not with his legs. He should have asked me to do it. Jumble would have helped.

At least Felix has got someone holding the ladder. Mr. Aitken, the chemist, who sometimes kindly delivers Felix's prescriptions.

"What are you doing?" I say to Felix, which is a pretty dumb question because it's obvious what he's doing, but I'm dreading why he might be doing it.

"Thought I might as well use the ladder," says Felix, "seeing as you went to all the effort of putting it up."

"And," says Mr. Aitken, "seeing as we've got a bit of a fire situation."

I stare at him. The smell of smoke is much stronger out here in the wind.

"Potential fire situation," says Felix. "So I'm just taking precautions."

Felix gives Mr. Aitken the kind of look grown-ups give each other when they're reminding each other not to scare children.

Too late.

I'm terrified.

"Don't worry yourself, dear," Mr. Aitken says to me. "There is a fire, but it's two valleys from here, past the other side of town. The wind's blowing it away from us, so we'll be all right. The fire teams have got it surrounded. They'll put in fire breaks, and it'll burn itself out."

Mr. Aitken's son is a volunteer firefighter, so I hope Mr. Aitken knows what he's talking about.

But what if he doesn't?

The hot smoky wind is swirling all around us.

"No need to panic, babushka," says Felix. "But we do

have to be alert. They say the thermometer's going to explode today, which could make this wind even fiercer."

I am panicking.

"That storm last night," I say. "Why didn't the rain put the fire out?"

"Just an electrical one," says Mr. Aitken. "Dry as a duck in a drought. Wrapping but no gift."

I should offer to go up the ladder so Felix doesn't have to risk his legs. But I'm feeling sick and dizzy, and there's something even more urgent I need to do.

I take Jumble into the living room.

"You have to stay here," I tell him in a low voice. "I need to go into town. You can't come with me. Only humans over ten can do what I have to do. Sorry, but that's the way it is."

Jumble looks at me mournfully.

I'm desperate to get away from the house before Felix and Mr. Aitken come in, but I owe it to Jumble to explain a bit more, specially now he's my sister.

"I started a fire," I say. "So I have to go and help put it out."

Now I have to get into town as fast as I can.

I have to find the people in charge of the firefighters and hope they'll let me train on the job.

They will if they're desperate for people to fight the fire. And if they won't let me volunteer, I'll explain I started it. They'll have to let me help then.

I run all the way down the hill to where our road joins the highway. I turn right and sprint toward town.

I've never run this far, not even on sports day at my old school when I volunteered to be in the thousand-meter race because I wanted to give Mum and Dad a trophy to take to Africa. Something to remind them of me if they get lonely.

I didn't win. All I got was a pain in the side.

It wasn't as bad as the pain I've got now. This one isn't just from running; it's from worry as well.

I try to cheer myself up. I picture what I hope I'll see

in the main street when I get there. A few weary but proud firefighters having a beer and polishing their fire trucks and congratulating themselves on a job well done.

A fire completely put out.

And when I confess to them that I started it, they'll be stern at first, but then they'll forgive me and explain it was actually quite good for them because they needed the practice.

Except I don't think that's going to happen.

A gleaming red blur roars past me on the highway.

A fire truck, heading toward town.

And another.

They must be coming from other areas. Extra trucks wouldn't be needed if the fire was completely out. Plus, if it was, all these black bits of soot wouldn't be flying around in the wind and sticking to my sweaty skin.

The pain in my side gets worse, and the smoky air is hurting my chest, but I try to run faster anyway.

I have another scary thought.

What if Josh was so hurt and angry about me being suspicious of him and sending him sprawling that he told people I lit candles in the forest? What if there are posters of me up all over town saying ARSONIST?

I'm close to the main street now. I slow down. I think about going back to the house and hiding with Jumble.

No. I started this and I have to help fix it.

I hurry round the corner into the main street.

Oh.

Oh, no.

The main street is full of fire trucks.

Eight, nine, ten, or more. Firefighters are running everywhere, shouting at each other and looking at maps and checking the equipment on their vehicles.

The fire must be big. That valley on the other side of town must be totally alight.

I squint into the distance.

I feel sick.

In the sky are big piles of smoke.

I go up to a firefighter who looks like he's supervising. He's got badges on his shirt, and he's yelling orders to a couple of fire trucks that are heading off.

"Excuse me," I say to him. "I want to volunteer."

The supervisor looks at me. He wipes his red face on a hanky and takes a swig from a can of soft drink. He gives me a stressed smile.

"Thanks, girlie," he says. "But we're all right, thanks. Why don't you run along and keep your mum and dad company, and maybe we'll call on your services for the next one."

I know why he's saying that.

All he can see is a short, skinny kid, dripping with sweat and covered in black bits. He doesn't know I'm desperate.

He doesn't realize how hard I'll work to make everything okay.

"I'm over ten," I say. "I'm old enough to volunteer."

The supervisor starts to explain that junior fire-fighting volunteers don't actually fight fires, and I get ready to tell him why I have to be allowed to.

Then something distracts us.

An ambulance has arrived with its siren going. It pulls over near us, and the siren stops, but its engine keeps running as if it's waiting for something.

A couple of people start yelling and pointing to the other end of the main street.

A vehicle is driving slowly toward us. It's a fire truck with its headlights on. It looks different from the other fire trucks. It's grimy and battered, with so many black streaks and smudges all over it you can hardly see the red paint. The firefighters riding on the back are slumped and staring at the road.

All the chatter and yelling in the main street stops. People even stop coughing.

Everyone stands and watches silently as the fire truck pulls up next to the ambulance and one of the doors of the fire truck opens and the paramedics reach in and lift out a stretcher.

On the stretcher is a man in very badly burnt overalls. His hands and arms are bandaged. His eyes are closed.

Oh, no.

I can't watch anymore.

As the ambulance speeds away, its siren wailing again, I run.

But my eyes are blurry with shame and I bang into someone. He catches me before I fall. It's a man in firefighting overalls, except the top half is flapping around his waist.

"Sorry, love," he says. "In a hurry."

I start to apologize too, then I stop and stare.

He's wearing a T-shirt that says CARMODY'S PEST REMOVAL. Same as the T-shirt Josh wanted to give me to say sorry. A woman trots up with her overalls only half on too, and she's wearing one as well.

Then I see who else is with them.

Josh and Tonya.

Josh gives me a nervous smile, but he doesn't say anything because he's too busy coughing, and the woman is talking to him nonstop.

"Get the chickens inside," she's saying, "and hose the trees close to the house."

"Yes, Mum," wheezes Josh.

They hurry past me.

I follow them and catch up with Josh.

"If the fire gets too close," I say to him, "jump in your dam."

It's all I can think of to say sorry for how I treated him and to try and protect him from what I've done.

"Thanks," he says, and coughs some more.

Mr. and Mrs. Carmody haven't noticed me, but Tonya is giving me an angry accusing glare.

Does she know?

Is she going to yell out in public? Tell everyone how all this chaos and panic and air pollution and serious injury and putting parents in danger is my fault?

Suddenly I don't care if she does.

I just want to confess and apologize and do what I can to make everything okay.

But then I imagine everybody in town with Tonya's angry face, everybody in Australia, and I don't see how anything can be okay ever again.

I turn and run.

Now I just want to go back home to South Melbourne.

I don't want to be huddled by the dry river in this dumb town with black bits swirling into my mouth and tears dripping onto my knees.

I blame the Nazis.

If they hadn't terrorized Felix, he wouldn't have got bad legs, and he could have come and looked after me at our house.

And if the Nazis hadn't murdered Felix's parents, he wouldn't have needed a birthday picnic to cheer him up. And I wouldn't have accidentally set fire to the district. And caused a brave firefighter to be badly burnt and poor Josh to be coughing his guts out when he can hardly breathe properly at the best of times.

A gust of hot smoky wind flings dust and soot into my eyes.

I know what the wind is telling me.

Don't blame other people for your own mistakes.

I turn my back to the wind and try to ignore it. I realize I'm crouched in a familiar spot. In front of me is something I recognize.

A small mound of dirt.

The poor bush mouse's grave.

Which is definitely not my fault. In fact, I don't reckon any of this is completely my fault. I reckon the first Zelda should start taking responsibility for some of it.

Okay, she was incredibly brave and determined. Okay, she was clever, loving, and never lost hope. Yes, she knew how to cheer Felix up when he needed it. Yes, she even knew how to cheer chickens up.

But didn't she ever stop to think how being perfect was going to make things difficult for other people?

How Felix would never get over her death?

How I'd be named after her and spend my life being secondhand and second best?

No, I don't think she did.

"Babushka."

I look round.

Felix is hurrying toward me. Behind him in the picnic area his car is parked with the door open and the engine running.

"Are you all right, babushka?" he calls.

He's breathless and worried and hobbling with his stick as fast as he can.

I don't know what to say. I want to be on my own. I don't want to have to say anything.

But when Felix reaches me, I throw myself into his arms and confess everything.

"I set fire to your thank-you letters," I sob. "Then I set fire to the district."

Felix stares at me.

Gently he wipes my face with his shirt sleeve.

"Come on," he says. "Come and sit in the car and tell me properly."

I do.

I tell him about the birthday picnic and Josh and the wind and the candles and how I last saw the thank-you letters disappearing into the sky in flames.

"I'm sorry," I say. "When the fire's out, I'll write to all your ex-patients and apologize. And to the family of the firefighter with the burnt hands. And I'll spend the rest of my life trying to make up for what I've done."

"Oh, babushka," says Felix, "you didn't start the fire. It started two valleys away. It was probably a lightning strike."

It's kind of him to try and make me feel better, but he's wrong.

"You didn't see how many letters there were," I say.

"You probably haven't looked at them for years in that old folder. When I got them out to cheer you up, there were heaps of them and they all caught fire."

Felix sighs but he doesn't say anything else.

He just gives me a long hug, then makes sure my seat belt is done up.

We drive away.

Felix is incredible. He's not angry or yelling at me or making me feel guilty or anything. I think he just wants to get me to a safe place. Maybe our house in Melbourne, where I can write my apology letters without people accusing me and throwing things at me.

He is so kind and loving.

But I can also imagine what he's thinking.

Mum and Dad once told me that Felix spent time with Russian troops in the last weeks of the war. That sounded pretty interesting, so I asked Felix what it was like. He didn't want to talk about it much. All he said was he made some friends, and one of the Russian words they taught him was *babushka*.

I asked him what it meant. He told me it was the nickname of a brave and daring woman in Russian history.

At the moment, he's probably wondering if it also means stupid idiot.

Now I'm confused.

We're heading in the wrong direction.

I haven't said anything to Felix because I don't want to distract him from his driving.

But if we're making a getaway to our place in South Melbourne, why are we going in the opposite direction? I've just seen a signpost. It says Melbourne that way, behind us.

Ahead of us, in the sky, are the big piles of smoke.

"Felix," I say, "why are we driving toward the fire?"

He doesn't answer.

His hands are trembling as he steers. For a sec I think he might be getting angry after all, then I remember his medical condition.

"Don't worry, babushka," he says. "We're only going a short way."

That's a relief.

So is the tone of his voice. He still doesn't sound angry at all. Which is amazing. There aren't many grandfathers who would sound this calm when their granddaughter has just started a bushfire.

Just thinking that makes me want to cry again.

I wipe my eyes and try to think of other things.

"Have you taken your pills?" I say.

Felix's hands are shaking pretty badly.

"I've run out," he says. "Jim Aitken was so keen to tell us about the fire, he forgot to bring any. I was going to ask you to take the prescription into town. Then somebody from the CFA rang to say you were already there and looking upset."

"Sorry," I say quietly.

"You don't have to be sorry, babushka," says Felix. "Of course you were upset."

He slows the car down and swings it into a carpark. We stop in front of a small tin building with a huge aerial on the roof and the letters *CFA* painted on the door.

"Where are we?" I say.

"Local bushfire command center," says Felix. "We're going to talk with the fire chief."

I stare at the building.

The fire chief?

Why?

Dread flickers inside me.

At my last school, some parents handed their kid over to the police after he stole chocolate marshmallows from a shop. Mum said it was called tough love, but she didn't think she could do it.

I don't reckon Felix would do it either. Except maybe to a hospital administrator.

"Why do we need to talk with the fire chief?" I say, nervously.

"Come on," says Felix. "You'll see."

We get out of the car.

Felix looks like he's on a mission, so we must be going to help in some way. Perhaps give the fire chief a clue about where the fire started.

I know Felix wouldn't tell on me, but this is pretty risky.

I can feel my insides coiling up with stress.

Calm down, Zelda, you're not a fire hose.

Inside the bushfire command center, it's even hotter.

There are big fans going, but they're just making a hot wind like the one outside.

Several people in firefighter shirts with sweat patches on them are standing around a table talking urgently into big mobile phones, which are crackling like old-fashioned radios from the 1990s.

The distant voices on the other end of the phones all sound like they're shouting.

The computers on the table have maps on their screens, and the printer is printing all the time, and the table is covered with pieces of paper.

There are a lot of used mugs too, all empty. I decide to be helpful and start making up for what I've done.

"Would anyone like more tea?" I say.

Nobody replies. Which I understand completely. When you're the command center for a bushfire, you've got more important things to think about.

"Excuse me," says Felix. "Who's in charge?"

A couple of the firefighters glance at him but don't stop talking into their phones.

Felix waits. You probably learn really good patience hiding in a hole for two years.

Finally a woman comes out of a back room carrying an armful of drinks. She sees us, dumps the drinks, and hurries over.

"Sorry, you two," she says. "You can't come in here. This is an operations center."

I wait for Felix to relax the mood by saying he's an expert at operations. But he doesn't.

"I appreciate you're busy," he says to the woman. "But I'd be grateful if whoever's in charge could take a moment to quickly reassure my granddaughter about something."

I look at Felix.

Aren't we meant to be telling them stuff?

The woman is looking at him too. Crossly.

"We don't have time for this," she says.

"I'm sorry," says Felix. "But it's important."

I can see he's not going to give in. Which is sort of fair. Mum reckons he always had time for anxious parents outside his operating room.

The woman goes over to a man on the other side of the room with lots of badges on his shirt. She says something to him apologetically.

The man gives us an irritated look and comes striding over.

"I'm in charge," he says.

"Could you please show my granddaughter where the fire started?" says Felix.

The fire chief rolls his eyes. Then he stabs his finger into the middle of a big map on the wall.

"Round about there," he says.

"And how far away is that from the forest near Lofty Road?" says Felix.

Now I'm confused.

What is Felix doing?

The fire chief is looking very annoyed.

I'm not surprised. He'd be worked off his feet if every local resident came in asking how far away the fire is from their house.

"A long way," snaps the fire chief.

"One more question," says Felix. "How far can a burning letter travel in a strong wind?"

The fire chief doesn't reply. He just gives a disgusted snort and starts to turn away.

Felix looks disappointed. Then determined.

He picks up a cigarette lighter from the table, and a piece of paper, and sets fire to the edge of the paper.

The fire chief stares at him, gobsmacked.

I'm feeling the same.

Felix holds the burning paper up and launches it into the hot breeze from the fans so it floats across the room in flames.

Everyone is staring now, mostly with their mouths open.

The burning paper floats down to the floor on the other side of the room, and after a few more seconds, the flames die away.

Just ash on the floor.

"Okay, you joker," explodes the fire chief. "That's it. Out."

"See, babushka?" says Felix to me. "Burning letters can't travel fifty kilometers. Not alight."

I stare at the ash on the floor.

"Which means," says Felix, "you didn't start the fire."

I want to hug him.

I want all the firefighters in the room to hug him.

I want to tell them they've just seen the kindest and most loving thing a grandfather has ever done.

But I don't because the fire chief is yelling at us.

And then suddenly one of the other firefighters is yelling even louder.

"Gav, listen to this."

The fire chief goes quiet and turns to him.

"Units sixteen and twenty-three have just called in," says the firefighter. From his face I can see it's bad news.

"The wind's changed," says the firefighter. "Totally. It's swung right round. The fire front's heading for the western exit road. They reckon an hour if we're lucky."

I glance around the room. Everybody's looking like it's definitely bad news.

Then I work it out for myself.

The western exit road must be the highway out of town that goes west, toward Melbourne. It's called Cairn-killey Road, and it runs past the bottom of Lofty Road.

Which means the news is really bad.

Lofty Road is the road to Felix's place.

I look at Felix.

"Sorry to trouble you," says Felix to the fire chief.

Then he grabs me and hurries me toward the door. I can see he's having exactly the same thought as me.

Jumble.

Now. We have to get home now.

We drive back toward town with the windows closed and the air-conditioning on full. I can see smoke in the sky ahead of us.

It wasn't there before.

Not on our side of town.

Jumble must be terrified.

Felix doesn't usually drive fast. It's not a good idea when you've got shaky hands. But now I want him to pretend he's a tank.

Drive over things.

Smash through things.

Anything so we can get to Jumble before the fire.

"Can't we go faster?" I say.

"We're not much use to anyone if we crash," says Felix.

"Anyway, they said the fire would probably take an hour to get to our place."

He reaches over and squeezes my shoulder.

"That was a very brave thing you did, babushka," he says. "Volunteering to fight the fire. Taking responsibility for what you thought you'd done. I'm proud you're my granddaughter."

I feel myself glowing, and it's not from the hot wind and smoke.

I'm so lucky to have Felix for my grandfather. I could have spent the rest of my life thinking I'd started this fire. Even after all the trees had grown back and the injured firefighter's arms had healed and I'd said sorry to everybody and given the firefighter some skin moisturizer, I'd still have felt guilty.

Felix has saved me from that.

I wish there was something I could do in return.

The main street is in chaos. Vehicles are parked everywhere. Not fire trucks this time. Family cars and people movers and trailers piled high with furniture and big-screen tellies.

People are running across the road, shouting at each other and talking on phones. I can see somebody on the roof of the post office holding a hose and peering into the distance. The ladies from the cake shop are stacking cakes in the back of a truck.

Normally Felix would stop and help them, but not now.

He drives close to the shops to get past them, which isn't easy, because the wind is rocking the car and the air is full of swirling black soot.

Up ahead people are getting onto the school bus, which is strange because it's Sunday.

"They've started evacuating," says Felix.

I know what evacuating means. I've seen it in war movies. It's when people don't want to stay, so they get out.

I'm puzzled.

"Why don't people want to stay and fight the fire?" I say. "Protect their homes and trees and stuff?"

"Some do, some don't," says Felix. "It's a personal choice."

I think about this. If people get scared, I don't blame them. Not everybody has a grandfather like mine.

Felix stops the car behind the school bus.

I'm about to remind him that we have to keep going when I see we're outside the chemist.

"I'll run in and get your pills," I say. "And some throat lozenges, in case the smoke gets really bad while we're defending the house."

Felix shakes his head.

"I want you to get on the bus," he says.

I stare at him.

"I mean it, babushka," he says. "I'll be okay. I've got hoses at the house and lots of buckets, and the gutters are clear. And if things get too bad, I'll evacuate as well, with Jumble."

"No," I say. "I want to stay with you."

I give him a determined look so he can see it's my personal choice.

Felix shakes his head. He grips my shoulders.

"I can't let you," he says. "I can't let it happen again."

He takes out his wallet and pushes some money into my hand. Then he leans across and opens my door.

"Go," he says.

He looks even fiercer than the fire chief did.

Stunned, I get out of the car.

"Go to the South Melbourne house," calls Felix. "You've got a key, right? I'll come and collect you when all this is over. I love you, babushka."

"I love you too," I say.

I just want to get back in the car, but I can see Felix doesn't want me to.

I start walking miserably toward the bus.

What did Felix mean, he can't let it happen again?

I don't understand.

Then I do.

I remember something Mum and Dad told me.

Something that happened seventy years ago, when Felix was put on a train to a Nazi death camp. Zelda could have gone free, but she wanted to stay with Felix. So she bit a Nazi officer, and she was put on the train too.

She would rather be with the person she loved than be safe.

Just like me.

But there's one important thing that's different, and I want to tell Felix what it is.

I turn back to the car. Felix is sitting there. I've never seen him look so miserable.

I get back in the car.

"I'm not her," I say.

We sit looking at each other, and I can see Felix is having a really big struggle deciding what to do.

"Poor Zelda was killed," I say. "But that doesn't mean I will be."

Felix looks at me some more.

He looks at the bus.

He opens his mouth to say something, but before he can, the bus drives away.

"Anyway," I say, "there's been too much leaving in our family and not enough staying."

Felix still doesn't say anything.

I can see he's still having the struggle.

"I can't leave Jumble," I say. "He's my sister."

That's probably not the best argument anybody's ever come out with, but because I'm lucky and Felix is a grown-up who listens to other people instead of just himself, he does a really good thing.

He puts the car into gear and we head off again.

The traffic on Cairnkilley Road is terrible. A long line of cars and trucks is heading out of town. We have to slow down.

Felix looks concerned, but he's not panicking, so I don't. He must be used to emergencies. The number of times he must have cut a person open and reached inside and found something he wasn't expecting. A lump of cancer. An extra kidney. A plastic mouthguard.

I want to show him I can be good in emergencies too.

"I didn't have a shower this morning," I say. "So there'll be even more water in the tank."

Felix nods.

"Good positive attitude, Margaret," he says. "Five out of five."

He switches on the wipers to get rid of the black bits that are settling on the windscreen now we've slowed down.

Except they're not just black bits anymore, they're black flakes.

Black glowing flakes.

Some of them have got little flames on them.

Lots of them have.

It's raining fire.

Felix squirts the windscreen and makes the wipers go faster. Some of the cars ahead of us pull over to the side of the road. Their wipers mustn't be as good as ours.

As we drive past, Felix winds down his window.

"Don't stop," he yells at them. "Keep moving."

I'm not sure if they hear us.

Felix has to close his window quickly when the burning flakes start coming in.

He glances back at the stopped cars and shakes his head.

"Never slow down when you're being attacked from above," he mutters. "Very bad idea, Margaret. Nought out of five."

"Did you learn that in the war?" I say.

Felix nods.

"Here we are at last," he says.

It's a relief to get off the highway and onto Lofty Road, where there's no traffic at all. As we speed up the hill toward the house, I see that the burning flakes are getting bigger. They're sounding more solid as they ping and clatter against the car roof.

I wonder if Felix feels like he's in the war now. I

don't ask him because it doesn't help to dwell in the past.

It's like me and Zelda. I could feel jealous of her, but what's the point?

She's not here, and I am. And I'm the one who's going to help Felix save Jumble and our house.

"**Now**, Jumble. Come out now."

My throat is hurting from yelling in this smoke. The swirling flakes of ash are stinging my face. I'm nearly fainting from the heat inside this sweater. But I carry on anyway.

"Jumble, don't be frightened."

I take a breath through the wet towel I'm holding over my mouth, then yell, then put the towel back.

"Jumble."

I don't get it.

Why would Jumble be hiding out here in the carport or the wood pile or wherever he is when he could be safe indoors? But he's not indoors. I checked all his hiding places, including under Felix's bed and in my school bag. I even checked the fridge, because he's always trying to get in there.

I could understand if Jumble was in his hole near the chickens. He does most of his digging when me and Felix are out. But he's not there either.

"Jumble," I yell again.

I squirt the hose everywhere I think he might be, like under the veranda and inside the barbecue, partly to stop those places catching fire and partly because Jumble hates water, so it'll encourage him to come out.

"Jumble."

I'm also having to squirt lots of places he probably wouldn't be, like up trees and in the birdbath, because the wind is blowing millions of red-hot embers. Small fires are breaking out all over the place.

I spray my sweater and towel, like Felix told me to. But breathing still hurts. And my mouth tastes of burnt cakes.

"Come on, Jumble."

Felix is yelling to Jumble as well, and spraying with two hoses at the same time, which is worrying me a bit. Without his stick, he's pretty wobbly. But when a grandfather's that brave, what can you say to him?

"Under the eaves," yells Felix.

It's hard to hear in this wind, but I realize he's yelling at me. He's pointing up under the edge of the roof. For a sec, I think Felix has seen Jumble up there, hanging by his claws, practicing being a smoke detector.

But it's not Jumble, it's a dark patch where the wood is

blistering and smoking. Suddenly flames burst through. Embers must be piling up in the gutter and making the metal so hot that the wood is burning.

I squirt the burning wood, and when it's out, I do the same to the gutter.

But only for a moment.

My hose goes limp, and the water stops.

I peer through the smoke. Felix's hoses have stopped too.

"Power's off," yells Felix.

That's a big problem.

Our water pump runs on electricity.

"I'll switch to the diesel generator," he shouts.

As Felix hobbles past me on his way to the water tank at the back of the house, he puts a mop in my hand. I know why. We did fire plans on my first day at the new school. Thank goodness Felix had time to get his plan ready before he came into town to find me.

I need two hands for the mop, so I wrap my wet towel round my head and face. I jam the mop into the nearest bucket of water and then splat it down onto the front door-mat, which is smoking badly.

The wind is so strong I can hardly stand up.

"Jumble, where are you?" I yell.

The wind blows my words away in a stinging spray of red-hot grit.

Something drops onto the veranda behind me with a thud. I turn round, hoping it's Jumble, even if he's fainted from the heat.

It's not. It's a bird.

I don't think it's fainted. I think it's dead.

I touch it gently with my foot. It doesn't move. Its beak is open. So are its eyes. Smoke is coming from its feathers.

Thud.

Another one drops into the front yard.

Thud.

Thud.

Thud.

They're all around me, just dropping out of the sky. There are so many, I can't stand it.

"Felix," I scream.

But he probably can't hear me in this roaring wind. And in this swirling smoke, he probably can't even see what's happening.

Oh, no.

One of the birds on the front lawn is moving.

What should I do? If it's injured and in pain, I should try to help it. But what can I do in the middle of all this? Should I try to put it out of its misery? I don't know if I can.

I take a fearful step toward the injured bird, which

is bigger than all the others and moving quite a lot, particularly its tail.

Tail?

I take another step. The tail wags.

"Jumble," I scream.

He looks at me through the smoke haze, then turns back to the dead birds, sniffing them with a puzzled expression on his face.

I pick him up and hug him. He licks my face, the bits he can get to. I loosen the wet towel so he can get to a bit more.

"We were worried about you," I say. "Where were you?"

He doesn't have to reply. In front of me is Felix's wheelbarrow, upside down on four bricks. Jumble must have been under there.

"Clever hiding place," I say.

Jumble gives me an uncertain look.

Something whacks me in the back so hard I stagger and fall onto my knees, still clutching him. For a sec, I think a fire truck has driven into me.

Then I realize it was a gust of wind, because another one comes and the wheelbarrow does cartwheels across the front yard and smashes into the side of the house.

We need shelter.

I have to get Jumble indoors.

Except I'm meant to be putting out fires. Where's my mop?

I glance round for it.

Something sharp and painful bounces off the side of my head.

It's a burning twig.

Frantically, I duck down and slap myself to make sure I'm not alight. More burning twigs hurtle past us. So do leaves and sticks and clumps of burning grass. I should have done what I was told when Felix ordered me to put on two of his sweaters. One's not enough protection against fiery missiles.

Keeping as low as I can and holding Jumble to my tummy, I crawl toward the house.

I reach the veranda.

This is the risky part. I have to stand up to get into the house.

"Hold on," I say to Jumble, and I glance behind me to see if it's all clear.

It's not.

The sky is black with smoke and ash, but I can see more twinkling clouds of burning bits hurtling toward us. I fling myself down and wriggle under the veranda with Jumble. I cover his ears as the twigs and sticks crash against the woodwork above us.

I hear another sound.

Breaking glass.

Jumble whimpers, and I almost do too. Even without looking, I think I know what that sound means.

I peek out from under the veranda.

I'm right.

The living-room window has broken, and swirling storms of burning bits are blowing into the house.

Now I wish I had my mop.

I've got to find a way of putting out these fires in the living room.

The one on the couch looks the most urgent. I grab the vase of flowers the survivors gave Felix for his birthday and hurl the water onto the flames.

It helps, but it's not enough. Flames jump up again. Jumble barks at them, which is good of him, but it isn't enough either.

The inside of the house is filling up with smoke from all the small fires and from the hot wind blasting in through the broken window. My eyes are stinging, but I can see well enough to spot any buckets of water that are sitting around.

There aren't any.

"Felix," I yell, "I need water."

Where is he? I haven't seen him since he went to get the diesel pump going. He must be having trouble with it.

I dash into the kitchen to see if Felix filled the sink with water as part of his fire plan.

No, he didn't.

Or the laundry sink.

Or the bath.

"I bet he would have," I say to Jumble. "If he hadn't been called away into town because of me."

I'm coughing so much, at first I'm not sure if Jumble can understand what I'm saying. But he gives a gentle growl, which I know is his way of telling me not to blame myself. Then he does a pee, which is a clever idea, except he's not doing it on any flames.

I realize he's trying to tell me something else.

The toilet. Of course. There's water in the toilet bowl and in the cistern.

I grab the toothbrush glass and tip out the toothpaste and brushes. I start scooping water out of the toilet and throwing it onto the small fires that are flaring up in the hallway. I do the same with the water in the cistern.

It works really well until the water runs out.

Jumble, who's eating the toothpaste, does a burp.

It makes me remember Felix's ginger beer.

"Thanks, Jumble," I say.

I stumble through the smoke to the cupboard in the laundry.

When Felix was a kid in his hiding hole, he used to get thirsty during the day because Gabriek could only bring him drinks at night. So Felix made a promise to himself that if he survived, he'd always have plenty of drinks handy.

And he does. He makes the ginger beer himself, twenty bottles at a time.

Yes. Fourteen bottles left in the cupboard.

I use three on the couch, and that does the job.

The air in the house is so hot that the towel round my head is dry and the bottle opener is burning my hand. I drench the towel with ginger beer. I wrap a kitchen cloth round my hand and drench that too. I drench Jumble.

"Sorry," I say as he yelps and gives me an indignant look.

Then I get back to the fires.

I use four bottles on the rug, two on the coffee table, two on the window frame, and the last two and a half on some flames that are creeping toward the violin hanging on the wall. Felix doesn't play it, but he cares about it a lot because it belonged to Gabriek.

I save a swig of ginger beer for me and one for Jumble.

"We're winning," I say to him.

Jumble gives a warning bark.

I look round.

Flames are coming through the ceiling directly above the bookcase.

I reach for the ginger beer and remember there's none left. Anyway, you don't spray ginger beer around books.

I lunge forward to snatch all the Richmal Crompton William stories and run with them to safety. Before I can, bigger flames spurt through the ceiling.

I jump back.

The flames are getting closer to the William books. I won't be able to fit the whole set into my arms. I'll need several trips to rescue them, and there's not enough time.

I feel my way back into the kitchen, grab some tea towels, open the fridge, and soak the cloths with whatever I can get my hands on, which is orange juice, milk, beetroot slices, pineapple chunks, beef curry, and the liquid that tofu comes in.

As I stumble back into the living room, I wonder what meal Felix will make with the leftovers on the floor.

The flames are all round the bookcase now. I swat at them with the wet cloths. The heat is so bad I can't really get close enough, but I have to because the edges of some of the books are starting to curl and smoke.

I can barely breathe and I can't see much now but I keep on swatting at the flames.

In the distance, I hear Felix telling me to stop, but I won't.

Felix didn't give up when he was a kid.

I can put this fire out.

The bookcase starts to topple. I try to get out of the way but I can't and the whole thing is falling onto me, burning books sliding off the shelves and crashing into me as I fall backward.

I'm on the floor, books all over me.

I can taste ash.

I can smell my hair burning.

"Felix," I scream, "help."

Sharp corners are stabbing into me and I can feel hot pains on my shoulders and legs.

Am I going to burn with the books?

Suddenly my arm is almost yanked out of its socket. Felix is dragging me out away from the pile of books and beating at my clothes with a very sticky tea towel.

Smoke curls up from the legs of my jeans.

Felix smothers them and pulls me to my feet.

"I'm sorry," I croak. "I'm sorry I couldn't save your books."

"You tried, babushka," he says. "Come on. The diesel pump's had it. We've got to get out of here while the car's still in one piece."

I'm still a bit stunned from having a bookcase fall on me and my head is foggy with smoke, so it takes me a moment to realize what he means.

Then I do.

He means leave the house.

Evacuate.

"No," I say. "We have to stay and fight."

Mum and Dad will never forgive me if they get back and find I've let Felix's house burn down. I'll never forgive myself.

Felix grabs me by the shoulders. His eyes are red and streaming. I can't tell if it's from sadness or the smoke.

"Babushka," he says, "you did your best."

He hugs me very tightly.

Then he picks up Jumble and pushes him into my arms and leads us out of the house.

I frantically try to think of things to grab.

Gabriek's violin.

The photo of Felix with the prime minister.

Zelda's locket.

Jumble's bowl.

Too late. We're outside. The car isn't burning. Felix grabs the handle of the passenger door and lets go of it straight-away, swearing and blowing on his hand.

I go to lend him the towel from my head, but when I reach for it, it's not there. The screaming wind has torn it off me.

Felix pulls his sweater sleeve over his hand and reaches for the car door again.

Then he stops.

He half turns and stares.

He's looking at something behind me, and whatever it is, his face says he can't believe it, he's never seen anything like it, not in all the years he's spent looking at things other people never even get a peep at.

I turn round.

I can't believe it either.

The sky is full of fire.

We're on the top of a hill, and sometimes we see planes flying in the distance and it feels like we're higher than the planes are.

There are no planes on the horizon now.

Just fire, as high as we can see.

Coming toward us.

"Quick," yells Felix, and pulls me and Jumble back into the house. We dash into our bedrooms and grab quilts and towels and blankets.

I have to do it by feel. The smoke is so thick it's almost dark in here. And the wind outside is so loud I can't hear anything I'm doing.

I wonder if Felix has remembered to grab Zelda's locket from under his pillow. I'd better remind him. Except I can't find the doorway to his room.

I don't know which way to go.

I don't know where Felix is.

I'm lost.

"Felix," I yell, "where are you?"

Jumble, who's bundled up in the bedding in my arms, licks my face, but it's not enough to stop the panic and the choking.

Then I feel an arm round me.

Felix is guiding me to safety.

We hurry out the back door into a blast of boiling hot air. We stagger across the backyard toward the chickens.

I stop.

Oh.

The chickens are just lying there. The wind is making their feathers flap, but apart from that, they're not moving.

"I'm sorry, babushka," shouts Felix into my ear. "I couldn't save them. All we can do now is try to save ourselves."

He goes into the shed.

Does he mean we should take shelter in there? I'm not sure if that's such a good idea. The shed is made of wood, like the house.

Felix comes out of the shed carrying two spades.

He hands one to me in the swirling howling orange and gray haze.

"We've still got a chance," he yells.

He clambers down into Jumble's hole and starts digging.

Jumble leaps out of my arms and into the hole and starts digging next to Felix.

For a moment, I stare at them both.

Felix is my grandfather. I love him, and I trust him. He's not panicking and weeping, so I'm not going to either.

I jump into the hole and start digging too.

Now. I want the screaming to stop now.

"It's just the firestorm getting closer," says Felix into my ear.

In the darkness, he hugs me and Jumble even tighter, and we hug him tighter back.

It's all we can do, lying here trembling in this hole in the backyard. Hold on to each other and hope that the quilts and towels and blankets we've piled on top of us will be enough.

The screaming roar gets even louder. I've never heard anything so loud and scary in my life.

Well, only once.

The day Mum and Dad flew off to Africa. We said good-bye at the airport, and then Mum and Dad went through the doors that only passengers can go through. Felix saw how upset I was and did a really kind thing.

He got our taxi to take us to the fence at the end of the runway so I could watch Mum and Dad's plane take off and wave to them.

It took off right over our heads, screaming just like this firestorm.

Except this is louder. This sounds like a hundred planes diving toward our house all at once. This is what a war must sound like.

I'm scared.

I tell myself not to be. Felix is an expert at sheltering in holes. He's had more experience at it than anyone else I know.

"Felix," I say, my mouth close to his ear, "what will happen to people who don't have holes to hide in?"

He doesn't answer for a bit.

"Most people have left," he says. "I hope."

I hope so too. Or else have holes of their own. Perhaps, if they're lucky, ones that are deeper than this one.

It's getting very hot in here.

"Felix," I say, "I'm finding it a bit hard to breathe."

I feel him move. I think he's reaching for something. It's not easy because there's only just enough room in here for two of us lying side by side. Jumble is snuggled on my chest.

Felix wriggles around some more. I hope he's not

trying to dig this hole bigger with his hands, because he'll hurt his fingers.

Suddenly a bright light shines in my eyes.

I squint, and Jumble gives a whimper of alarm.

"It's okay," I say to Jumble when I see what it is. "It's just a flashlight."

Jumble probably thought it was the firestorm.

Felix is opening a leather medical-type bag, which I didn't even know he had with him. He must have grabbed it from his room with the quilts and stuff.

He reaches into it, which isn't easy, because it's between his feet. But he manages. He takes out a plastic bottle of water, and we all have a sip. Then he drags out a red metal cylinder. It's got a rubber tube with a little yellow plastic mask on the end.

"This is oxygen," says Felix. "When you find it hard to breathe, put the mask over your mouth, and it'll help."

I put the mask over my mouth.

Felix turns a knob on the cylinder, and, he's right, it does help.

I take the mask off.

"Can Jumble have some?" I say.

We give some to Jumble.

"Okay," says Felix. "Let's save the rest for later. And I'll turn the flashlight off to save the battery."

In the darkness, I wonder why Felix didn't have any of the oxygen himself. Perhaps he had some before when he was trying to get the diesel generator started.

I stay as still as I can.

I try to be calm and wait for the fire to pass. I may not be brave and heroic like Zelda, but at least I can practice being patient.

Except now the firestorm is screaming even louder, and I've never been so hot.

I feel myself starting to panic.

"Felix," I say, "tell me a story."

When I was little and I used to ask that, he always used to read me a story from a book. Which is strange, seeing as he's so good at telling real-life stories.

We haven't got a book in here, so I hope he can think of a real-life story now.

"What story would you like?" says Felix.

"A story about people in danger," I say. "People who are patient and survive."

I wait for Felix to start.

He must be thinking.

"And their dog survives too," I say.

With his mouth to my ear, Felix tells me a story.

It's about a boy called Wilhelm, a girl called Violetta, and their dog called Jumble. A fire breaks out in their cake shop, and they're in great danger. But kind grown-ups called Barney and Genia and Gabriek take care of them and keep them safe.

"Does Gabriek play his violin?" I ask.

"Yes," says Felix quietly.

Me and Jumble have some more oxygen, and Felix finishes the story. It has a happy ending. The children are saved, and so are the cakes.

That's amazing.

I'm pretty sure Felix made some of that up. And I always thought he didn't have a good imagination.

"Thanks," I say to Felix. "I like stories like that. Stories about good protection."

Good protection is what me and Mum and Dad say when somebody gives somebody else protection that's brave and loving and good.

Felix is quiet now. Is he thinking up another story? Then in the darkness, he starts to shake. For a horrible moment, I think he's having trouble breathing.

But he's not.

He's crying.

"What is it?" I say. "What's the matter?"

I can be so dim sometimes.

Being in this hole must be so much harder for Felix than for me and Jumble. For me, it's just a scary new experience. And Jumble has always wanted to have his hole this deep. But for poor Felix, it must be like being buried in sad memories.

I grope around, trying to find the cylinder so Felix can have some oxygen. I'm hoping oxygen isn't just good for breathing, I'm hoping it's good for sadness too.

Before I can find it, Felix starts telling me another story.

He squeezes the words out between sobs.

It's about a boy and a girl in Poland in 1942. The boy is Jewish, and the girl is Polish, and they're best friends.

Felix doesn't have to tell me their names. I know who they are.

The boy is worried that the girl is in terrible danger. If the Nazis catch her with him, they'll think she's Jewish and kill her too. He tries everything he can to keep her safe. Finally, he can only think of one more thing.

To protect her, he has to leave her.

"So the boy wasn't there when the Nazis caught her," says Felix, his voice almost a whisper in my ear. "And they hung her. They put a rope round her neck and hung her in the town square."

I didn't know that.

I close my eyes but I can still see it.

I've got tears of my own now.

It's the saddest story I've ever heard. It's also the best

good protection story I've ever heard. Even if it does have a sad ending.

Poor Zelda.

I'm eleven, and look how scared I am.

She was only six.

I snuggle even closer and hold Felix as tight as I can without squashing Jumble.

"Felix," I say, "you did your best."

Now what's happening?

I think I've been asleep.

The screaming noise is going away. I can still hear it, but it's in the distance. There are other sounds above us, creaking, cracking sounds, but compared to the terrible screaming roar, it's almost like silence.

Does this mean we've survived?

As soon as I have that thought, I have another one.

My phone.

It's in my pocket.

If the firestorm has passed, I can ring emergency and get someone to come and rescue us.

If only it wasn't so hot and smoky in here. I can hardly keep my eyes open. Jumble is asleep on my chest. I can hear him snoring. I think Felix must be asleep too, because he's not crying anymore, or saying anything.

I'm so sleepy I can't remember what I was going to do.

Oxygen.

If I have some oxygen, I can think better.

I fumble in the darkness and find the bag and grope inside it, but the oxygen cylinder isn't there. Just some other things in little crackly packets.

Snacks?

I fumble around some more and find the torch and switch it on and stare at the things. They're not snacks. They're syringes.

Why would Felix bring syringes? Why would he want to give injections down here? Injections are to make you better or to knock you out. That doesn't help in the middle of a fire.

I don't understand, but I do remember what I have to do.

Ring for help.

I wriggle my hand into my pocket and pull out my phone.

So hot in here.

So sleepy.

I feel like I've already had a knock-out injection.

Why am I holding my phone?

I can't remember.

I press the keys.

Dead.

Now I have to wake up.

A voice is telling me to. And a cool breeze wants me to as well. It's making the wetness on my face feel cold. My skin doesn't feel sleepy anymore.

"Babushka," says the voice. "Babushka."

I open my eyes.

Jumble is licking my face.

Behind him, leaning over me, looking very concerned, is Felix.

I'm hot. I sit up and take off a sweater. Felix helps me.

"I've been asleep," I say.

"You have," says Felix, looking relieved. "Are you burnt anywhere?"

I shake my head. I can feel a couple of sore places from where the books fell on me, but that seems like ages ago.

"That's a relief," says Felix. "We're all okay, then."

It's so nice to see them both. But I'm feeling confused. I don't know where I am. When I went to sleep, I was in a hole in the backyard near the house and we had a pile of quilts and towels and blankets over us.

I'm still in the hole, but I can't see the quilts and towels and blankets.

I can't see the house either.

Felix helps me stand up. My legs are shaky.

"Take it easy for a moment," he says. "We were in here for quite a while. My legs were a bit wobbly as well when I came to."

I look around. I see the quilts and towels and blankets in a pile next to the hole. What's left of them. They're mostly black and ragged. But at least they're there.

The house isn't.

It's gone.

All that's left, scattered on the ground, are bricks and chunks of burnt wood and twisted sheets of roof metal and lots of little sooty things I don't recognize, but I think they used to be parts of bigger things.

That's bad enough, and I know I should spend some time getting used to it, but I don't. I look around, farther into the distance.

Oh.

My legs give way, and Felix catches me.

It's not just the house that isn't there.

Nothing is.

The front yard isn't, and the front fence isn't, and the mailbox isn't, and the forest isn't. All I can see in the smoky haze are a few black tree trunks, and most of them aren't even standing up.

Which I wouldn't be either, if Felix wasn't holding me. It's like something out of an awful dream. And not just because the smoke has turned the sunlight a strange color.

I take a few deep breaths of smoky air. It hurts my throat. But that's okay, I'm used to that by now.

It's everything being gone I'm not used to.

I can see Jumble feels the same. He wants to jump down from Felix's arms and sniff around, but Felix won't let him, and I realize why. There's ash everywhere under our feet, and some patches of it are still hot. Me and Felix have got shoes on, but Jumble hasn't.

I know. I'll get the scissors and the stapler and one of Felix's leather place mats and make Jumble some little—

No, I won't.

The scissors and the stapler and the place mats are all probably gone too. I can't see the fridge anywhere, and if a firestorm can make a fridge disappear, I'm pretty sure scissors and staplers and place mats wouldn't stand a chance.

Or violins.

Or photos.

Or bedrooms.

Or lockets.

I take Jumble from Felix and hide his face in my T-shirt so he won't get too upset when he sees his bowl is gone.

And when he sees how upset I'm getting.

"Your house," I whisper to Felix. "Your lovely house."

Felix puts his arms round me and Jumble.

"I know," he says quietly.

I can see how upset he is.

I wish I could help him feel better.

"At least we're all okay," I say to him. "Thanks to you."

"And Jumble's hole," says Felix.

I think Jumble reckons it's thanks to me, from the adoring way he's gazing at me and putting his tongue up my nose.

But I know the real-life story.

Now we're sitting on the remains of the quilts and towels and blankets on what used to be our front steps.

Waiting.

I wish we could go into town. I want to make sure everybody else is okay. The firefighters and Josh and the other kids in my class. And I need to see if the phone outside the post office is working. My mobile isn't, and I want to call Mum and Dad.

Jumble wants to go as well. He's got friends in the district he's worried about too. Dogs and the people in the butcher shop and wombats.

But Felix won't let us.

"It's still too dangerous," he keeps saying. "The ground's too hot. Burning trees are still falling. We have to wait."

I stare at what used to be the forest. The trees used to be taller than the house. Now they're mostly lying on the ground, black and split and smoking. It's like a disaster movie, except without the film stars.

We're the only living things here.

"If we went into town," I say, "we could be careful and watch out for falling trees."

Felix shakes his head.

"Huge, smoldering fires could be hidden under the ash," he says. "If you trod in one, it would burn your legs off."

Sometimes I wonder how Zelda managed to do so many brave things with Felix being so cautious and so careful.

"We could watch out carefully for all the hidden smoldering fires," I say.

Okay, Felix knows about legs, but I know a bit about fires. I did almost start one.

"Be patient, babushka," says Felix.

It's hard being patient. I'm starving and really thirsty. Our water bottle is empty. Our water tank has gone.

Jumble is thirsty too. I can tell by the way he's panting and not dribbling like he usually does. And Felix is licking his lips a lot and his tummy is making very hungry noises.

"Can't I even look for food?" I say.

Felix shakes his head again.

"We have to wait for things to cool down," he says. "Anyway, babushka, there isn't any food left here."

He's probably right. Most of the food in the house wouldn't have survived the heat. But the popcorn might.

A gust of breeze blows hot stinging ash into my face.

"Ow," I say.

I don't say anything else.

I don't cry. I try to be as brave and determined as I can.

Okay, I do cry a bit.

Jumble licks my face, and Felix puts his arm round me.

"I know how you feel," he says. "I want to make everything okay too."

He's right. That is what I want to do.

And I can't.

I give Felix a hug to show him I'm sorry for being grouchy with him.

"When I was a kid," says Felix, "I lived in a cellar for a bit with some other kids. We got miserable and hungry sometimes, and that's when we made a story tent."

"A story tent?" I say. "What's that?"

"We mostly did it with coats," says Felix. "But blankets work just as well."

He grabs a couple of blankets and puts them over us so they make a tent. It's hot inside, but cozy. I can tell Jumble likes it. And it's good not having to look at the disaster movie.

"Okay," says Felix. "Now we tell each other stories."

We take it in turns.

We're both very careful not to have food or missing

parents in our stories, because stories are meant to make you feel better, not worse.

Felix tells me an amazing one about what happened to him after the war. He and Gabriek worked together for years, mending houses that had been blown up in battles. Each evening, Gabriek drank wine to help him stop thinking about his wife, Genia, who the Nazis had killed. Each evening, Felix went to the library and read medical books because he wanted to be a doctor. But he couldn't get into university in Poland. So Gabriek brought him to Australia, where there were more opportunities.

"Wow," I say. "What a kind man."

"Yes," says Felix quietly.

"What happened to him?" I say.

"He lived in Melbourne," says Felix, "until he got old and died."

Thinking about Gabriek gives me an idea for a real-life story.

I tell it to Felix. It's about a man who feels bad because he couldn't give enough good protection in the war to someone he loved. But then, later on, he is able to give good protection to somebody else, and he feels better.

When I finish the story, I realize Felix hasn't made a sound for ages.

I look at him to check he's listening.

He is.

Now I can see the vehicle more clearly through the smoke haze.

A small truck, driving along Lofty Road.

I jump up and wave.

"We're over here," I yell at the truck. "We want to be evacuated."

"Stay on the steps, babushka," says Felix.

I yell and wave at the truck some more. Felix gets to his feet and does the same.

When the truck reaches where our front gate used to be, it turns off the road and heads toward us.

"Yes," I shout excitedly. "We're going to be rescued."

But as the truck gets closer, I'm not so sure.

I can't see anything on it that says POLICE or CFA or STATE EMERGENCY SERVICE. And it hasn't got any tires on its wheels. It's bumping over what used to be our driveway on its metal rims.

Which I guess is more than our car could do. Our car's wheels have melted.

The windscreen of the truck is so cracked, I can't see who's inside.

It pulls up, and the door creaks open.

There's only one person in there.

I stare. Suddenly I don't feel excited anymore. Just surprised. And disappointed.

It's Tonya.

She slumps forward on the steering wheel and stares at us. Her face has got ash on it. And two trickle marks where tears have been running down her cheeks.

"Josh is dying," she says.

Felix hurries over to her. I do too.

"Who's Josh?" Felix asks Tonya.

"My brother," she says. "He can't breathe."

For a sec I wonder why she's come all this way on really bad suspension to tell us instead of staying with Josh. Then I see she's pointing to the back of the truck.

Lying on a partly burnt mattress is Josh. He looks like he's unconscious. He's got ash all over him, and he's wheezing worse than ever.

Felix hurries to the back of the truck and Tonya gets out and follows him.

"Does he have any burns?" says Felix, peering at Josh.

"I don't think so," says Tonya. "A roof tile hit him in the chest when our house exploded. We were in the dam."

Felix gently touches Josh on the neck and chest.

Even under all the ash on him, I can see that Josh's face is a strange color. Sort of a bit blue.

"Has he always had breathing problems?" says Felix.

Tonya nods.

"Asthma," she says.

Felix looks even more worried than before.

"Wait here," he says.

He goes over to what used to be our steps and grabs his medical bag. I wish he'd asked me to get it. Then I wouldn't have to be standing here with Tonya, both of us staring at the ground.

Felix comes back and leans over the side of the truck. He carefully loosens Josh's shirt and listens to Josh's chest with a stethoscope. Then, still listening, he gently taps Josh's chest several times with his fingertips.

I can tell from Felix's face he doesn't like what he's hearing. He puts his stethoscope away and turns to Tonya.

"What's your name?" he asks.

"Tonya," she says, looking scared.

I don't blame her. When a doctor treating a relative asks your name, it can mean bad news.

"You were right to come here, Tonya," says Felix. "The smoke has made your brother's asthma very bad. And his injury from the roof tile has made things worse. Fluid is building up in his chest cavity. He needs an operation as soon as possible."

I stare at Josh, wondering what I can do. I wish he was conscious so I could tell him that one of Australia's best surgeons is going to help him.

Except if he asked, I'd have to tell him I don't know how. There's nothing left here to do an operation with. We haven't even got scissors or a stapler.

Tonya is looking at Felix, taking in what he said. She's not screaming or panicking or fainting.

Although I don't like her, I'm impressed. If somebody told me a member of my family needed an operation as soon as possible, and I didn't have any tires, I don't know what I'd do.

"Tonya," says Felix, "do you know if the hospital is open?"

Tonya shakes her head.

"I came straight here from our place," she says.

Felix turns to me.

"Check your phone again, babushka," he says.

I check it. Still no signal.

I shake my head too.

Felix puts his medical bag onto the passenger seat of the truck.

"The hospital's a brick building," he says. "It might still be open. There's only one way to find out."

Now. I want Josh to take another breath now.

I brace myself in the back of the truck as we drive round a big fallen tree. I give Josh's hand an encouraging squeeze. Tonya does the same with his other hand.

Josh takes a breath, but it's a very wobbly and wheezy one.

It's probably not helping that he's bouncing up and down so much. His mattress has got springs, which is good and bad. Felix is driving carefully, but the road is covered with burnt bits of trees, and it'd be bumpy even if we had tires.

I glance into the front of the truck. I bet this is not easy for Felix's legs either. Oh well, at least he's got Jumble with him. If his legs get too painful, Jumble will lick them.

We bump over another branch and Josh jolts up and

down again, but he still doesn't wake up. Poor kid. A person would have to be pretty sick to stay unconscious through all this.

"It's okay, Josh," says Tonya, stroking his head. "We'll be at the hospital soon."

I decide not to say that it'll probably be a while. We're not at the bottom of Lofty Road yet, and with these wheels, we won't be able to speed up even on the highway.

I give Josh's hand another encouraging squeeze. No point worrying him, even though he is unconscious.

I'm watching his breathing closely, like Felix asked me to.

I'm also trying not to look at Tonya. It's very stressful being here with someone who's only just given up her hobby of bullying me.

At last. We're turning onto the highway.

Oh.

Oh, no.

That car at the side of the road. It's totally burnt. The people in it aren't moving. They look like they're burnt too.

I look away.

Josh. I should be watching Josh. Is his breathing getting slower, or am I imagining it?

I try not to get distracted again, but a bit farther on, there are two cars that have crashed into each other. They're both burnt as well. As we drive past, I can't see any people in them, but next to one is a pile of ash with something sticking out of it.

I think it's a pair of glasses.

Oh.

Tonya isn't taking her eyes off Josh. I don't think she saw the burnt cars. It's best if she doesn't.

Out of the corner of my eye, I see more burnt cars ahead.

I decide to try and make conversation. Even talking to a bully is better than thinking about what's in those poor cars.

"Where are your parents?" I say to Tonya, keeping my eyes on Josh.

"They went out this morning on the fire truck," she says, sounding miserable. "I haven't heard from them since."

I don't know what to say next.

Perhaps talking wasn't such a good idea.

"I'm sorry," says Tonya quietly.

I'm not sure what she means. When I glance up, she's looking at me with a really unhappy face.

"I'm sorry I called you those dumb things," she says. "And took your grandfather's present. And I'm sorry those other two were so mean to you."

I still don't know what to say.

Yes I do.

It's not that simple, I want to say.

You can't bully someone and then just apologize because your brother's sick and your house exploded and your gang's been evacuated and you need help.

I decide to say it.

Before I can, Tonya blurts out more.

"The only reason I picked on you," she says, "was to get the heat off Josh."

I try to work out what she means. The fire hadn't even started when she first picked on me.

Tonya is gazing sadly at her brother. She smooths his hair away from his eyes, which are still closed.

"The other kids in the class always made fun of Josh," she says. "I wanted to give them someone else to make fun of instead."

Now I understand.

"So they'd leave Josh alone," I say.

Tonya nods.

I can't believe it. That is so ruthless. Tonya must have rubbed her hands in glee when I arrived, a short kid with an unusual name and an unusual family. Imagine how pleased she'd have been if she'd known there are two of us.

"What about us?" I want to say. "I bet you didn't stop to think how we'd feel."

Oops, I did just say it.

Tonya is staring at the floor of the truck. She looks really ashamed of herself.

We both remember Josh at the same time. We look at him and hold our breath until he takes a breath himself.

I hope we get to the hospital soon, and not just for Josh's sake.

Me and Tonya have run out of things to say, and this conversation is feeling really awkward.

Except the truck is going even slower now.

In fact, we're stopping.

I look at the road ahead and see why.

The highway is blocked by a huge fallen tree. On both sides of us, in what used to be the forest, massive tangles of logs half buried in ash are glowing fiercely. If we try to drive cross-country, we'll cook.

There's only one thing to do.

Now it's my turn.

"Five minutes is up," I say to Felix and Tonya. "It's my turn to carry Josh."

At least my phone's good for one thing. It still won't make calls, but the clock's working.

Tonya ignores me. Just keeps plodding with Josh on her back.

"Felix," I say, "it's five minutes."

Felix is walking next to Tonya with his hand on Josh's neck pulse. He's listening carefully to Josh's breathing.

"Let Tonya carry on if she can manage," says Felix. "She's bigger than you."

That's not fair. People should be allowed to help even if they aren't as big as other people.

Up ahead is the last bend in the highway before town, so the hospital's still about fifteen minutes away. It's better if we take turns rather than Tonya getting exhausted and dropping Josh.

I look at Jumble for support. I don't get any. Jumble is happy in my arms. He doesn't like being carried by Tonya, and I think he gets jealous when I carry Josh.

Sisters can be a bit selfish sometimes.

Oh well, at least Felix isn't trying to carry Josh. Which is good. When we get to the hospital he'll need all the strength he's got left to supervise Josh's operation.

"How are your feet?" I say to Felix as we plod on.

"Four out of five," he says.

I think they're probably worse than that. My feet are really sore from this hot road, and I've got thick rubber soles on my new boots. Tonya is wearing boots as well. But Felix's shoes have got thin leather soles, and they're almost burnt through.

I'm glad he thought of stuffing pages from the truck service manual inside them before we set off.

Hey, why is Tonya speeding up?

If she tries to walk that fast, she'll definitely get exhausted. And Felix won't be able to keep up. I've told her he's got bad legs.

"Tonya," I say, "slow down."

She ignores me again.

And goes even faster.

I think she's showing off, trying to impress Felix. She

hasn't got a hope of keeping that speed up all the way to the hospital.

I knew it, she's slowing down.

And stopping.

And letting Josh slide off her back.

"Tonya," I yell.

Felix drops his medical bag and catches Josh, and I rush over and take part of the weight. Felix takes Jumble from me, and I get Josh onto my back.

What is Tonya playing at?

Then I see she's not playing at anything.

She's running over to a burnt-out fire truck half hidden by fallen branches at the edge of the highway. Most of the paintwork is blistered, but not the name of the sponsor written on the bottom of the fire truck door.

CARMODY'S PEST REMOVAL.

"Mum," Tonya is screaming. "Dad."

It's awful.

Even from here, I can see there's nobody in the fire truck. Not even blackened bodies. Just ash, all around, still smoking.

Tonya reaches out to yank the fire truck door open.

"Tonya," shouts Felix. "Don't."

Too late.

Tonya grabs the big metal door handle with both hands

and screams even louder. She staggers back, clenching her hands in agony. Then she sinks to her knees, sobbing.

Felix grabs her and pulls her back onto the highway. He brushes the ash off her legs and looks at her hands. I can tell from his face she's got burns.

"Mum," she's sobbing. "Dad."

"Tonya," says Felix gently, "we don't know for sure what's happened to them. So let's just think about what we do know. We have to get Josh to the hospital."

Tonya nods through her tears.

Which is pretty brave, I think.

I look at Tonya for a moment, confused thoughts swirling inside me. I've got tears in my eyes too.

I keep hold of Josh on my back with one hand and put my other arm round Tonya.

Just for a moment.

I think it's what Zelda would have done.

Now we're in town.

I can't believe it.

The main street looks like it's been bombed.

All that's left is rubble and smoke and ash and tangled wire and twisted sheets of metal and bits of wood that look like they used to be shop signs. The mobile phone tower that used to be on top of the post office is lying on the road, and there isn't a post office anymore, just bricks.

Bricks everywhere.

Black.

And burnt bodies.

Oh.

I look at the bricks instead. Which I don't understand. I get why all the wooden houses have gone, but bricks are meant to be strong. They're meant to be fireproof. You make fireplaces from bricks, so why is the post office gone?

And the video shop.

And the hardware shop.

And Mr. Aitken's chemist shop, where we were going to get some cream for Tonya's hands.

Even Jumble looks like he's in shock. He was enjoying being carried in Felix's medical bag. Now he's whining and staring at the rubble where the butcher shop used to be.

Poor Tonya does a loud sob, even louder than the ones she's been doing all the way into town.

Her parents' shop is gone too.

Then I see the worst thing. At the other end of the main street. Right under where the sun is big and red behind the smoke.

The hospital.

Gone.

Felix gives a loud groan.

We just stand here, stunned.

I don't know how much longer I can keep Josh on my back. He keeps slipping, and each time it's harder to hang on to him.

Two people, a man and a lady both covered in soot, come slowly toward us through the rubble. As they get closer, I see they've hardly got any clothes on.

"Is there an emergency hospital?" says Felix to them. "An emergency medical center?"

They look at us for ages as if they don't understand the question. Then the man shakes his head and they move slowly away.

I know what Felix is thinking. I've seen it on TV. After disasters, the army arrives in huge helicopters with food and drink and bandages and portable operating equipment, and they set up emergency medical tents.

I look around.

No army.

No helicopters.

No tents.

The few people I can see don't look like they could help us set up an emergency medical center. They're mostly dazed or crying or hunting through the wreckage of houses, calling people's names.

Felix checks Josh's pulse and his breathing, and gives another groan, a quieter one this time. I've never seen Felix look so exhausted.

"I think we're losing him," says Felix.

My first thought is to make sure Tonya didn't hear that.

She didn't. She's standing on the other side of the street, staring at where her parents' shop used to be.

I look around at what used to be the town, trying to think what else we can do. Now. Before it's too late.

Suddenly I see something glinting on the hillside above

where the hospital used to be. The whole hillside is black except for one strip of green. One little unburned patch of trees.

It's like a memory of how the town used to be.

And in that one green gully, sunlight is glinting off a window.

"Felix," I say, "could you do the operation in a house?"

He looks at me, and for a while he doesn't seem to understand the question.

I point.

Felix looks up the hill.

Because he's so exhausted, he needs time to think about it.

Then he nods.

Now we've got a problem.

We're inside the house. The power is off. So is the water.

"Doesn't matter," says Felix.

We drink from the toilet cistern.

The windows in the bathroom are small, and not much daylight is getting in, so Felix decides the kitchen is the best place for the operation.

There's another problem.

Felix hasn't got any of his pills.

Silently I beg his hands to stop shaking. But they don't. And Felix can't start operating on Josh until they do.

I ask him if aspirin or vitamins will help. He says no. And I can't find any other medicine in the kitchen or in the bathroom. Only antiseptic cream and Band-Aids.

All we can do is finish the preparations.

And hope.

Carefully, we lay Josh on his back on the kitchen bench. We take his shirt off.

I find some disinfectant under the sink and pour it into a bowl with some cistern water. We wash Josh's chest with it, as gently as we can because Josh is hardly breathing.

At least when a person's unconscious, you don't have to worry about tickling him.

"Knife," says Felix.

I check all the knives in the drawer. The sharpest one is a small fruit knife, which Felix says will be big enough.

"Tubes," says Felix.

He explains we need two tubes. One must be non-bendy and about as wide as my thumb. The other must be bendy and about as wide as my finger.

Under the sink Felix finds a plastic funnel with a non-bendy nozzle.

"This'll do," he says.

We look everywhere in the kitchen for a bendy tube and don't find anything until I spot one attached to the juicer.

"Good girl," says Felix.

The tube is stained orange with juice, but Felix says that won't matter.

I disinfect the knife and the tubes. Felix disinfects his hands, scrubbing them with a vegetable brush.

They're still shaking.

Please, I say to them silently, just stop for five minutes.

But they don't, and when Felix checks Josh's breathing, I can tell from both their mouths it's almost too late.

Josh's is blue. Felix's is desperate.

Felix stares at his trembling hands, and I can see him thinking of the thousands of times he's been able to depend on them in the past. And how much he wishes he could now.

I have a thought.

I try to make it go away by concentrating on the sound of Tonya sobbing in the next room, where she's lying down with antiseptic cream on her hands, like Felix told her to.

When that doesn't work, I try to block out the thought by listening to Jumble complaining that dogs shouldn't be locked in bathrooms when people's lives need to be saved.

When that doesn't work, I tell my thought to Felix.

"I could do it," I say quietly.

Felix looks at me.

"If you tell me how," I say.

Felix frowns, and for a fleeting moment I think he's going to put me in the bathroom with Jumble.

Instead, he hands me the vegetable brush.

"While you scrub up," he says, "I'll tell you a story."

It's a real-life story about the time Felix was in the

Polish forests with the partisans in 1945, after he had to leave his hiding hole.

"Gabriek joined the partisans to fight the Nazis," says Felix, "and took me with him. I couldn't fight because of my legs, so I became an assistant to one of the doctors. And one day we had so many wounded, I had to take bullets out of people myself."

I stare at Felix. That's amazing. He was only a couple of years older than me.

"Keep scrubbing," says Felix, glancing anxiously at Josh.

"Sorry," I say, and plunge my hands back into the bowl of disinfectant and scrub my fingernails even harder.

"Before I made my first cut into a wounded man's leg," says Felix, "the doctor gave me a piece of advice. He said, don't think about mistakes you've made in the past. Don't worry about what might happen in the future if this goes wrong. When your blade cuts into the skin, just think about now."

Felix looks at me, and I nod.

I understand that story.

"Pick up the knife," says Felix.

I pick up the fruit knife.

Felix points with a wobbly finger to the side of Josh's chest.

"See that pimple next to the bruise?" he says.

"Yes," I say.

"I want you to push the knife in just below the pimple," says Felix. "Push it in until the first letter of the brand name on the blade is level with the skin. Then make a cut to just above that mole. The one there, halfway down the bruise."

I stare at the blade and the pimple and the mole.

"Understand?" says Felix.

I nod.

"Now," says Felix.

For a second or two, my head fills with thoughts of bush mice and me at Josh's funeral in handcuffs.

I make the thoughts go away.

I push the knife into Josh's chest.

It only goes in a bit.

"Harder," says Felix.

I push harder. The knife goes in a bit more.

Then suddenly it slips in easily. I stop before the brand name touches the skin.

My hand is wet with blood.

I hesitate.

"Now," says Felix.

I cut down to just above the mole.

"Knife out," says Felix.

I pull the knife out.

Blood is everywhere now. And so is Felix. He pushes a

finger into the cut and makes the hole bigger. He pushes the nozzle of the funnel into the hole and slides the bendy tube into the funnel. He puts his ear to Josh's chest and jiggles the tube into Josh bit by bit until suddenly something gushes out of the tube.

More blood.

Much more blood.

Felix snatches up a plastic bucket and lets the blood gush into it.

I think I'm going to faint. When Felix told Tonya that Josh had a buildup of fluid in his chest, he didn't say anything about the fluid being blood.

Felix is looking at me, and his eyes are shining.

"I'm so proud of you," he says.

Why? I want to scream. We've killed Josh.

I wish I could go back into the past. To before I did this terrible thing. To before I ever tried to be brave and determined.

But I keep quiet. And an amazing thing happens. The gushing blood stops. Josh does several big hiccups and some very big gasps.

And suddenly I'm glad I'm here with Felix.

I'm glad we're not in the past.

Because Josh is breathing now.

"**Now**," says the medical officer to Tonya. "If you don't get on the helicopter now, it'll leave without you."

I can see Tonya doesn't want to.

She wants to stay here in the big emergency medical tent and keep looking for her parents. I don't blame her. I would too.

Even Josh wants to keep looking for them, and he's on a stretcher.

"You have to go," says Felix gently to Tonya and Josh. "But don't worry. The moment your parents turn up, we'll let you know."

"We promise," I say to them.

"Woof," says Jumble, which means he guarantees we will.

Josh and Tonya don't look happy.

I understand why.

There are hundreds of people wandering around these tents, mostly hoping family members will turn up. But not all of them will. Not with so many poor burnt bodies all over the district.

I don't know what else to say to Tonya, so I just give her a hug.

"Tonya," yells a voice.

I feel her go stiff and tense.

"Daddy!" she screams.

She flings herself at an ash-covered man. I recognize what's left of his CARMODY'S PEST REMOVAL T-shirt. And the one his wife is wearing as she drops to her knees to hug Josh.

"Oh, love," says Mrs. Carmody to him tearfully, "when we heard you weren't on the evacuation bus, we thought you were—" She stops and stares at Josh's bandages in alarm. "What happened to your chest?"

Josh points to me and Felix.

"Her granddad is a surgeon, and he saved my life."

Felix gives my hand a little squeeze. I give him one back. We've decided it's probably better if Josh and his family don't know that an eleven-year-old operated on him.

"Felix was brilliant," I say. "He inserted a drain tube between Josh's fifth and sixth ribs and straight through his intercostal muscles into his pleural cavity to relieve the pressure of the fluid."

I think I've got that right. I made Felix tell me so I'll know the details if I ever have to do it again.

Mr. and Mrs. Carmody thank Felix and tell him what a hero he is.

Felix shakes his head.

"You're very kind," he says. "But no."

He looks at the dazed and exhausted people. Firefighters helping each other with their burns. Family members crying together. Friends and neighbors with their arms round each other. Scared, bewildered people on their own. Strangers comforting other strangers.

Suddenly I realize what all these people are.

Survivors.

Felix goes over and speaks to a weary-looking man in a sooty firefighter's shirt.

It's the fire chief from the bushfire command center. Felix looks like he's apologizing about something. The fire chief stares at him for a long moment. Then he shakes Felix's hand.

Felix comes back over.

"Sometimes we get things wrong," he says to Mr. and Mrs. Carmody, "but we do our best."

He puts his arm round me.

"I learned that from my granddaughter," he says, "who did her best for Josh."

Mr. and Mrs. Carmody look at me gratefully.

"Thank you, love," says Mrs. Carmody, dabbing her eyes.

"Good on you, sweetheart," says Mr. Carmody.

Felix gives me a proud smile.

"I should have mentioned before," he says. "Her name's Zelda."

Now the ceremony has started, and I'm not feeling so sad.

We've had some sad visits to some sad graveyards over the past few weeks. The last one was yesterday when I went with Tonya and Josh to say good-bye to three of the kids from my class.

This one feels different.

I can see it's the same for everybody here. Mum and Dad and Felix's friends from the Holocaust survivors group.

This is such a good idea of Felix's. To give Zelda a memorial ceremony in this beautiful graveyard full of ferns that have sprung up since the fire. I think he got the idea when we were searching through the ashes of his bedroom and we made an incredible discovery.

Zelda's locket had survived.

Felix crouches by Zelda's memorial headstone and gently places her locket into the earth.

The look on his face is so lovely as he says a few words to her. I'm glad the rest of us are standing back a bit so he can say them in private. When you've had a friendship with someone for seventy years, you deserve a quiet moment between the two of you.

Then Felix turns to the rest of us.

"Would anyone like to say anything?" he asks.

Several people nod.

Dad thanks Zelda for looking after his dad.

Mum thanks Zelda for being a loving inspiration to our family.

Some of the people from the survivors group say some very kind and grateful things about non-Jewish people like Zelda and Barney and Genia and Gabriek, and all the help they gave to Jewish people who needed it.

Then Felix looks at me.

It's my turn.

I take a step closer to Zelda's little headstone.

"All my life," I say to her, "I've wanted a sister so much. And all along, without knowing, I've had one. I'm sorry I took so long to realize it was you."

I pause. When your sister died seventy years ago, a moment like this is very emotional.

Jumble pauses too. He stops sniffing the ferns and

gives me a grateful look. I can see how happy he is about going back to being a dog.

"You did so much in your life," I say to Zelda, "and I'm glad we've laid you to rest because you deserve it. I've hardly started my life, and there's heaps of things I'm planning to do, and after I've done them, I can't wait to come up here and tell you about them."

I pause again. Felix is gazing at me. His eyes are even softer than usual. He doesn't say anything, because he knows there's something else I need to say.

"You always spoke up bravely," I say to Zelda. "And now I'm going to give it a go."

I look at Mum and Dad.

I hope this isn't unfair, because I know they're not expecting this.

I say it anyway.

"In our family," I say, "there's something we do a lot. The parents always leave the kids. It happened to Felix, it happened to Dad, and it happened to me. I think we should stop it."

Mum and Dad stare at the ground.

Everyone does.

Nobody says anything.

Then Mum puts her arms round me.

"You're right," she whispers.

Dad hugs me too. He still doesn't say anything, but

he's looking at me with the same expression Ms. Canny gets when you give her an answer she wasn't expecting and she has to think about it.

I give Mum and Dad a smile, so they can see that speaking up doesn't mean you stop loving people.

We all gaze at Zelda's headstone for a while.

Jumble gives it a loving lick, and some of the people from the survivors group place small stones on it. Which is so nice of them all, because these are two different ways of saying she'll never be forgotten.

"We're lucky, aren't we?" I say to Felix. "To have her in our lives."

Felix puts his arm round me.

"Very lucky," he says. "And we're lucky to have you, Zelda. Your life is going to be very interesting, and I can't wait to see what you do with it."

Neither can I.

Suddenly I want to give a last grateful memorial whoop before I get started.

But I wouldn't do that in a graveyard.

Not even once.

Not even if I had written permission, not even then.

Oops, I'm doing it.

"Good one," says Felix. "Five out of five."

I can tell from his face he'd like to do that himself one day. He holds my hand and gazes up at the clear blue sky.

Suddenly I know what's going to happen next.

Felix has decided not to wait. He's going to do a big joyful whoop himself.

And he does.

Now.

Dear Reader,

Now *is the third book about Felix.*

In Once *and* Then, *Felix is a ten-year-old struggling to survive in Nazi-occupied Poland in 1942. He and his dearest friend, six-year-old Zelda, are caught up in that terrible time we call the Holocaust.*

If you haven't read Once *and* Then, *please don't worry. I've tried to write these stories so they can be read in any order. If you read* Now *first, you will know some of what happens in* Once *and* Then, *but not too much.*

I hope that after reading these stories, you may want to connect with real voices from the Holocaust. On my Web site is a list of books that contain some of those voices. I've also listed the books I read about Australia's catastrophic Victorian bushfires in February 2009.

I couldn't have completed this story without expert help. My thanks to Dr. Lionel Lubitz for his advice on all things pediatric, and to Danielle Clode and her husband, Mike Nicholls, for sharing some of their vast bushfire knowledge and expertise. Mike is the volunteer captain of the Panton Hill Fire Brigade in Victoria, and Danielle's book A Future in Flames *(Melbourne University Press, 2010) is a must for anyone who wants to know about bushfires in Australia.*

Finally, gratitude beyond words to a special group of people. Some work for Penguin Books, some for Henry Holt, others are close to me in other ways. They're a kind of extended family for Felix and the two Zeldas. No author gets things right all the time, and these fine aunts and uncles make sure no harm comes to my young characters if ever my judgment lapses. I'm lucky to have them.

morrisgleitzman.com

SQUARE FISH

DISCUSSION GUIDE

Now
by Morris Gleitzman

1. How is Felix the grandfather like Felix the child?

2. Which of Felix's characteristics are attributable to his experiences during the war?

3. In what ways are the lives of Zelda and her parents different from those of other families because of Felix's experiences?

4. Why does Felix react the way he does when his granddaughter gives him a copy of *William's Happy Days*?

5. Felix doesn't like being called a hero. Why? Do you think Felix is a hero?

6. How is Zelda and Felix's experience in the bushfire similar to the horrors Felix faced as a child? What memories might the fire have dredged up for Felix?

7. Can anything positive be gained from an event like the bushfire or what Felix experienced in the war?

8. Can it be dangerous to dwell on the past? Or to ignore the past? How?

GO FISH

MORRIS GLEITZMAN

Felix has a strong connection to the author Richmal Crompton. Are there any authors you connect to in the same way?

A few, but none more than Richmal Crompton and her Just William books. Which is why I made her Felix's favorite author. I was about eight when I discovered William on a library shelf. Suddenly I understood it was possible to be naughty and good at the same time. I rampaged with Richmal Crompton's golden-hearted naughty boy through thirty-four volumes of the funniest stories ever written. The more William tried to set things right in his world, the more he left behind him a trail of chaos and destruction and yelling adults, and the more I loved him. I catch glimpses of William in many of my own characters—even the cane toad ones.

Felix keeps Zelda's locket as a memento. Do you have any old family heirlooms or treasures?

I have a buttercup (now dried) that I picked from beside the railway tracks at Auschwitz when I first visited there before writing the Felix books. One of the things that strikes you when you go to a place like that for the first time is how ordinary it looks. I wanted the buttercup to remind me as I was writing these books that the Holocaust didn't all take place in some kind of expressionistic hell environment. Some of the horrors took place with the sun shining and the buttercups growing.

**There's an extraordinary line in *Then*: "I'm Zelda's evidence."
Tell us about that line.***

Felix's resolve is that he should survive and get back into the normal world. He's Zelda's evidence in that he can let the world know who killed her and why, but more importantly he's living evidence of who she was and what she embodied . . . her love.

Stories are really important to Felix. I wanted to write about something that I and all writers, certainly of fiction, know to be true—that not only is the imagination an infinite and powerful and wondrous place but it can be a place of refuge and consolation. It's also a great problem-solving laboratory; it's a place where we can rehearse aspects of our lives as well as fondly relive the past. We can encounter our own histories through our imagination and do a bit of a rewrite if that's what suits. For an ordinary working writer it's a huge part of daily life, and I've never forgotten how it's also a huge part of children's daily lives. Many of the creative processes that are part of my profession were part of my daily life as a kid.

Why did you choose to make Zelda the daughter of Nazis, rather than Jewish?*

There were a number of reasons I made Zelda non-Jewish. Felix and Zelda's friendship, the ten-year-old boy and the six-year-old girl, for me is the absolute heart of these books. Sometimes I get strange looks when I say that for me these are not stories about human hatred and cruelty and genocide; they are primarily stories about love and friendship. It was a very conscious decision to write about these things in the context of the complete opposite—the best our species is capable of surrounded by the worst we're capable of.

I wanted Felix and Zelda's friendship to cross the Jewish–non-Jewish boundary that condemned so many millions and that literally became a matter of life and death. Between these two kids it isn't important at all. Though in another sense it is, of course, because when Zelda starts identifying as Jewish, she doesn't fully understand the implication of that; she loves Felix and she wants to be what Felix is. So through her love she places herself at great risk.

Are you Jewish?*

I'm a bit Jewish. I'm always careful to acknowledge—even as I'm ordering another matzo soup—that my mother isn't Jewish. One of my grandfathers was a Polish Jew from Cracow. I know he left Poland as a young man early in the twentieth century. He and some other members of the family (I'm not exactly sure who) had been out of Poland for decades before World War Two, but some of the extended family remained there.

Where did the immediate family move to?*

London. My grandfather married a Jewish woman in London and had some kids, but she got sick and died. Then he married a non-Jewish woman, and my father was one of the kids of that second marriage. So he wasn't brought up in the Jewish faith, and my grandfather died when my father was about six. When I started thinking about these stories, it was a few years before I realized there was a distant family connection for me here, and maybe subconsciously that had been a part of it all along.

When I went to Cracow for the first time, it was really just as part of a holiday and not with any specific consciousness that I was researching this book. But as soon as I was there, on the streets of that town and in the Jewish cemetery and the fact that there was "Gleitzman" on a couple of gravestones and things, it suddenly started . . . I started to feel some connections.

It was only after I finished *Once* that I then did a fairly obvious calculation that I probably should have done earlier, and realized that if my grandfather had not left Poland and if my father had been born there, he would have been within a year or so of Felix's age, and that obviously has significance too.

I learned a long time ago that one can pretend to be the world's best researcher and to have the world's most muscular imagination, but the truth for me is that the protagonists of all my books, even the cane toads, are essentially me or aspects of me. I think fiction is always pretty autobiographical.

What challenges do you face in the writing process, and how do you overcome them?

Many challenges. In the Felix books I was very conscious of drawing fiction from real events that of course can only be truly known by people who experienced them firsthand. I've tried to make it clear in the author's notes that these are pieces of fiction very much inspired by real events. And I guess in subtler ways I tried to do that with the choice of titles. In *Once*, I started each chapter with the word "once" and I included one or two sentences in the past tense to remind readers that this does relate to a historical context, but then I moved into the present tense because it was very important to me to also remind young readers that history, for the people experiencing it, was the *now*. I used a similar device with the other Felix books.

What's your idea of fun?

Usually it involves emotion of some kind. Friendship. Sport. Nature. In particular, reading. In our lives we just don't get to go everywhere, do everything, be everyone, have every possible human experience, and spend most of the time excited, happy, scared, hopeful, amazed, sad, thrilled, inspired, amused, and tearful, with meal breaks. When we read stories, we do.

What are your hobbies?

See above. Plus travel, by plane or foot. And tea, especially Chinese tea, but not the floral swill most Chinese restaurants in the Western world give you. There are countless wonderful Chinese teas, and they can offer sublime complexities of flavor equal to the best wine. Plus, you can drink them all day at work without losing the ability to spell.

When did you realize you wanted to be a writer?

It started with the pleasure I got from a childhood filled with books and reading. And the discovery that in our imaginations anything is possible, even if you don't have heaps of money, big muscles, or permission to fly to Istanbul. Which in my childhood, to my indignation, I didn't.

SQUARE FISH

What advice do you wish someone had given you when you were younger?

I was given something better than advice. I was given a book. When I was fourteen, after being a passionate and tireless reader as a kid, I just stopped reading almost overnight. I got very interested in rock music and girls, and I mistakenly thought that books couldn't be part of the rock 'n' roll/girlfriend-filled lifestyle I aspired to. During that time, I left school, emigrated with my family to Australia (from England) and, at sixteen, was working in a clothing factory. One day, a guy who operated one of the cutting machines at the factory came up to me and said: "I've just finished reading this book and I think you might like it." It was *The Horse's Mouth* by Joyce Cary. The first paragraph reminded me of what language can do. By about ten pages in, I said to my parents, "I've taken a wrong turn and I want a life filled with books again." *The Horse's Mouth* is the book that I owe all my books to. That factory worker's random act of kindness changed my life.

What do you wish you could do better?

If only I could be as bold as Ben in my book *The Other Facts of Life*, as determined as Annie in *Second Childhood*, as optimistic as Colin in *Two Weeks with the Queen*, as indefatigable as Keith in *Misery Guts*, as big-hearted as Ro in *Blabber Mouth*, as inventive as Mitch in *Belly Flop*, as empathetic as Pearl in *Water Wings*, as imaginative as Angus in *Bumface*, as loving as . . . well, you get the picture.

What would your readers be most surprised to learn about you?

1. I have fourteen teapots.
2. My legs are disproportionately long in relation to my torso, and my head is disproportionately bald in relation to my dog.
3. In my work, I strive assiduously, tirelessly, and regularly to avoid, wherever possible, writing adverbially.

* Questions excerpted from an interview between Sophie Cunningham and Morris Gleitzman